Moran of The Lady Letty

A STORY OF ADVENTURE OFF
THE CALIFORNIA COAST :: ::

BY
FRANK NORRIS

AMS PRESS
NEW YORK

Reprinted from the edition of 1898, New York

First AMS EDITION published 1971

"Reprinted from a copy in the collection of the
Cleveland Public Library"

Manufactured in the United States of America

International Standard Book Number: 0-404-04790-4

Library of Congress Catalog Number: 75-144665

AMS PRESS INC.
NEW YORK, N.Y.   10003

Dedicated to

CAPTAIN JOSEPH HODGSON

United States Life Saving Service

Contents

Moran of the Lady Letty

Shanghaied

THIS is to be a story of a battle, at least one murder, and several sudden deaths. For that reason it begins with a pink tea and among the mingled odors of many delicate perfumes and the hale, frank smell of Caroline Testout roses.

There had been a great number of débutantes "coming out" that season in San Francisco by means of afternoon teas, pink, lavender, and otherwise. This particular tea was intended to celebrate the fact that Josie Herrick had arrived at that time of her life when she was to wear her hair high and her gowns long, and to have a "day" of her own quite distinct from that of her mother.

1   1

Moran of the Lady Letty

Ross Wilbur presented himself at the Herrick house on Pacific Avenue much too early upon the afternoon of Miss Herrick's tea. As he made his way up the canvased stairs he was aware of a terrifying array of millinery and a disquieting staccato chatter of feminine voices in the parlors and reception-rooms on either side of the hallway. A single high hat in the room that had been set apart for the men's use confirmed him in his suspicions.

"Might have known it would be a hen party till six, anyhow," he muttered, swinging out of his overcoat. "Bet I don't know one girl in twenty down there now—all mamma's friends at this hour, and papa's maiden sisters, and Jo's school-teachers and governesses and music teachers, and I don't know what all."

When he went down he found it precisely as he expected. He went up to Miss Herrick, where she stood receiving with her mother and two of the other

2

girls, and allowed them to chaff him on his forlornness.

"Maybe I seem at my ease," said Ross Wilbur to them, "but really I am very much frightened. I'm going to run away as soon as it is decently possible, even before, unless you feed me."

"I believe you had luncheon not two hours ago," said Miss Herrick. "Come along, though, and I'll give you some chocolate, and perhaps, if you're good, a stuffed olive. I got them just because I knew you liked them. I ought to stay here and receive, so I can't look after you for long."

The two fought their way through the crowded rooms to the luncheon-table, and Miss Herrick got Wilbur his chocolate and his stuffed olives. They sat down and talked in a window recess for a moment, Wilbur toeing-in in absurd fashion as he tried to make a lap for his plate.

"I thought," said Miss Herrick, "that you were going on the Ridgeways' yacht-

ing party this afternoon. Mrs. Ridgeway said she was counting on you.
They are going out with the *Petrel*."

"She didn't count above a hundred,
though," answered Wilbur. "I got your
bid first, so I regretted the yachting
party; and I guess I'd have regretted it
anyhow," and he grinned at her over his
cup.

"Nice man," she said,—adding on the
instant, "I must go now, Ross."

"Wait till I eat the sugar out of my
cup," complained Wilbur. "Tell me," he
added, scraping vigorously at the bottom
of the cup with the inadequate spoon;
'tell me, you're going to the hoe-down
to-night?"

"If you mean the Assembly, yes, I am."

"Will you give me the first and last?"

"I'll give you the first, and you can
ask for the last then."

"Let's put it down; I know you'll forget it." Wilbur drew a couple of cards
from his case.

4

"Programmes are not good form any more," said Miss Herrick.

"Forgetting a dance is worse."

He made out the cards, writing on the one he kept for himself, "First waltz—Jo."

"I must go back now," said Miss Herrick, getting up.

"In that case I shall run—I'm afraid of girls."

"It's a pity about you."

"I am; one girl, I don't say, but girl in the aggregate like this," and he pointed his chin toward the thronged parlors. "It unmans me."

"Good-by, then."

"Good-by, until to-night, about——?"

"About nine."

"About nine, then."

Ross Wilbur made his adieu to Mrs. Herrick and the girls who were receiving, and took himself away. As he came out of the house and stood for a moment on the steps, settling his hat gingerly upon his hair so as not to disturb the parting, he was not by any means an ill-looking chap. His good height was helped out by his long coat and his high silk hat, and there was plenty of jaw in the lower part of his face. Nor was his tailor altogether answerable for his shoulders. Three years before this time Ross Wilbur had pulled at No. 5 in his 'varsity boat in an Eastern college that was not accustomed to athletic discomfiture.

"I wonder what I'm going to do with myself until supper-time," he muttered, as he came down the steps, feeling for the middle of his stick. He found no immediate answer to his question. But the afternoon was fine, and he set off to walk in the direction of the town, with a half-formed idea of looking in at his club.

At his club he found a letter in his box from his particular chum, who had been spending the month shooting elk in Oregon.

"Dear Old Man," it said, "will be

back on the afternoon you receive this.
Will hit the town on the three o'clock
boat. Get seats for the best show going
—my treat—and arrange to assimilate
nutriment at the Poodle Dog—also mine.
I've got miles of talk in me that I've got
to reel off before midnight.

"Yours,

"JERRY.

"I've got a stand of horns for you,
Ross, that are Glory Hallelujah."

"Well, I can't go," murmured Wilbur,
as he remembered the Assembly that was
to come off that night and his engaged
dance with Jo Herrick. He decided that
it would be best to meet Jerry as he came
off the boat and tell him how matters
stood. Then he resolved, since no one
that he knew was in the club, and the
instalment of the Paris weeklies had not
arrived, that it would be amusing to go
down to the water-front and loaf among
the shipping until it was time for Jerry's
boat.

Moran of the Lady Letty

Wilbur spent an hour along the wharves, watching the great grain ships consigned to "Cork for orders" slowly gorging themselves with whole harvests of wheat from the San Joaquin Valley; lumber vessels for Durban and South African ports settling lower and lower to the water's level as forests of pine and redwood stratified themselves along their decks and in their holds; coal barges discharging from Nanaimo; busy little tugs coughing and nuzzling at the flanks of deep-sea tramps, while hay barges and Italian whitehalls came and went at every turn. A Stockton-river boat went by, her stern wheel churning along behind, like a huge net-reel; a tiny maelstrom of activity centred about an Alaska commercial company's steamboat that would clear for Dawson in the morning.

No quarter of one of the most picturesque cities in the world had more interest for Wilbur than the water-front. In the mile or so of shipping that

Shanghaied

stretched from the docks where the China
steamships landed, down past the ferry
slips and on to Meiggs's wharf, every
maritime nation in the world was rep-
resented. More than once Wilbur had
talked to the loungers of the wharves,
stevedores out of work, sailors between
voyages, caulkers and ship chandlers'
men looking—not too earnestly—for jobs;
so that on this occasion, when a little,
undersized fellow in dirty brown sweater
and clothes of Barbary-coast cut asked
him for a match to light his pipe, Wilbur
offered a cigar and passed the time of day
with him. Wilbur had not forgotten that
he himself was dressed for an afternoon
function. But the incongruity of the
business was precisely what most amused
him.

After a time the fellow suggested
drinks. Wilbur hesitated for a moment.
It would be something to tell about, however, so, "All right, I'll drink with you,"
he said.

The brown sweater led the way to a sailors' boarding-house hard by. The rear of the place was built upon piles over the water. But in front, on the ground floor, was a barroom.

"Rum an' gum," announced the brown sweater, as the two came in and took their places at the bar.

"Rum an' gum, Tuck; wattle you have, sir?"

"Oh—I don't know," hesitated Wilbur; "give me a mild Manhattan."

While the drinks were being mixed the brown sweater called Wilbur's attention to a fighting head-dress from the Marquesas that was hung on the wall over the free-lunch counter and opposite the bar. Wilbur turned about to look at it, and remained so, his back to the barkeeper, till the latter told them their drinks were ready.

"Well, mate, here's big blocks an' taut hawse-pipes," said the brown sweater cordially.

Shanghaied

"Your very good health," returned Wilbur.

The brown sweater wiped a thin mustache in the hollow of his palm, and wiped that palm upon his trouser leg.

"Yessir," he continued, once more facing the Marquesas head-dress. "Yessir, they're queer game down there."

"In the Marquesas Islands, you mean?" said Wilbur.

"Yessir, they're queer game. When they ain't tattoin' theirselves with Scripture tex's they git from the missionaries, their pullin' out the hairs all over their bodies with two clam-shells. Hair by hair, y' understan'."

"Pull'n out 'er hair?" said Wilbur, wondering what was the matter with his tongue.

"They think it's clever—think the women folk like it."

Wilbur had fancied that the little man had worn a brown sweater when they first met. But now, strangely enough, he was not in the least surprised to see it iridescent like a pigeon's breast.

"Y' ever been down that way?" inquired the little man next.

Wilbur heard the words distinctly enough, but somehow they refused to fit into the right places in his brain. He pulled himself together, frowning heavily.

"What—did—you—say?" he asked with great deliberation, biting off his words. Then he noticed that he and his companion were no longer in the barroom, but in a little room back of it. His personality divided itself. There was one Ross Wilbur—who could not make his hands go where he wanted them, who said one word when he thought another, and whose legs below the knee were made of solid lead. Then there was another Ross Wilbur—Ross Wilbur the alert, who was perfectly clear-headed, and who stood off to one side and watched his twin brother making a monkey of himself, without power and without even the desire of helping him.

This latter Wilbur heard the iridescent sweater say:

"Bust me, if y' a'n't squiffy, old man. Stand by a bit an' we'll have a ball."

"Can't have got—return—exceptionally—and the round table—pull out hairs wi' tu clamsh'ls," gabbled Wilbur's stupefied double; and Wilbur the alert said to himself: "You're not drunk, Ross Wilbur, that's certain; what could they have put in your cocktail?"

The iridescent sweater stamped twice upon the floor and a trap-door fell away beneath Wilbur's feet like the drop of a gallows. With the eyes of his undrugged self Wilbur had a glimpse of water below. His elbow struck the floor as he went down, and he fell feet first into a Whitehall boat. He had time to observe two men at the oars and to look between the piles that supported the house above him and catch a glimpse of the bay and a

glint of the Contra Costa shore. He was
not in the least surprised at what had
happened, and made up his mind that it
would be a good idea to lie down in the
boat and go to sleep.

Suddenly—but how long after his advent into the boat he could not tell—
his wits began to return and settle themselves, like wild birds flocking again after
a scare. Swiftly he took in the scene.
The blue waters of the bay around him,
the deck of a schooner on which he stood,
the Whitehall boat alongside, and an
enormous man with a face like a setting
moon wrangling with his friend in the
sweater—no longer iridescent.

"What do you call it?" shouted the red
man. "I want able seamen—I don't
figger on working this boat with dancing
masters, do I? We ain't exactly doing
quadrilles on my quarterdeck. If we
don't look out we'll step on this thing
and break it. It ain't ought to be let
around loose without its ma."

Shanghaied

"Rot that," vociferated the brown sweater. "I tell you he's one of the best sailor men on the front. If he ain't we'll forfeit the money. Come on, Captain Kitchell, we made show enough gettin' away as it was, and this daytime business ain't our line. D'you sign or not? Here's the advance note. I got to duck my nut or I'll have the patrol boat after me."

"I'll sign this once," growled the other, scrawling his name on the note; "but if this swab ain't up to sample, he'll come back by freight, an' I'll drop in on mee dear friend Jim when we come back and give him a reel nice time, an' you can lay to that, Billy Trim." The brown sweater pocketed the note, went over the side, and rowed off.

Wilbur stood in the waist of a schooner anchored in the stream well off Fisherman's wharf. In the forward part of the schooner a Chinaman in brown duck was mixing paint. Wilbur was conscious that he still wore his high hat and long coat, but his stick was gone and one gray glove was slit to the button. In front of him towered the enormous red-faced man. A pungent reek of some kind of rancid fat or oil assailed his nostrils. Over by Alcatraz a ferry-boat whistled for its slip as it elbowed its way through the water.

Wilbur had himself fairly in hand by now. His wits were all about him; but the situation was beyond him as yet.

"Git for'd," commanded the big man.

Wilbur drew himself up, angry in an instant. "Look here," he began, "what's the meaning of this business? I know I've been drugged and mishandled. I demand to be put ashore. Do you understand that?"

"Angel child," whimpered the big man. "Oh, you lilee of the vallee, you bright an' mornin' star. I'm reely pained, y'know, that your vally can't come along, but we'll have your piano set up in the lazarette. It gives me genuine grief, it do, to see you bein' obliged to put your lilee white feet on this here vulgar an' dirtee deck. We'll have the Wilton carpet down by to-morrer, so we will, my dear. Yah-h!" he suddenly broke out, as his rage boiled over. "Git for'd, d'ye hear! I'm captain of this here bathtub, an' that's all you need to know for a good while to come. I ain't generally got to tell that to a man but once; but I'll stretch the point just for love of you, angel child. Now, then, move!"

Wilbur stood motionless—puzzled beyond expression. No experience he had ever been through helped in this situation.

"Look here," he began, "I——"

The captain knocked him down with a blow of one enormous fist upon the mouth, and while he was yet stretched upon the deck kicked him savagely in the stomach. Then he allowed him to rise, caught him by the neck and the slack of his overcoat, and ran him forward to where a hatchway, not two feet across, opened in the deck. Without ado he flung him down into the darkness below; and while Wilbur, dizzied by the fall, sat on the floor at the foot of the vertical companion-ladder, gazing about him with distended eyes, there rained down upon his head, first an oilskin coat, then a sou'wester, a pair of oilskin breeches, woollen socks, and a plug of tobacco. Above him, down the contracted square of the hatch, came the bellowing of the Captain's voice:

"There's your fit-out, Mister Lilee of the Vallee, which the same our dear friend Jim makes a present of and no charge, because he loves you so. You're allowed two minutes to change, an' it is to be hoped as how you won't force me to come for to assist."

It would have been interesting to have followed, step by step, the mental process that now took place in Ross Wilbur's brain. The Captain had given him two

minutes in which to change. The time
was short enough, but even at that Wilbur changed more than his clothes during
the two minutes he was left to himself in
the reeking dark of the schooner's fo'castle. It was more than a change—it was
a revolution. What he made up his mind
to do—precisely what mental attitude he
decided to adopt, just what new niche he
elected wherein to set his feet, it is diffi-
cult to say. Only by results could the
change be guessed at. He went down
the forward hatch at the toe of Kitchell's
boot — silk-hatted, melton-overcoated,
patent-booted, and gloved in suèdes.
Two minutes later there emerged upon the
deck a figure in oilskins and a sou'wester.
There was blood upon the face of him and
the grime of an unclean ship upon his
bare hands. It was Wilbur, and yet not
Wilbur. In two minutes he had been,
in a way, born again. The only traces of
his former self were the patent-leather
boots, still persistent in their gloss and

shine, that showed with grim incongruity below the vast compass of the oilskin breeches.

As Wilbur came on deck he saw the crew of the schooner hurrying forward, six of them, Chinamen every one, in brown jeans and black felt hats. On the quarterdeck stood the Captain, barking his orders.

"Consider the Lilee of the Vallee," bellowed the latter, as his eye fell upon Wilbur the Transformed. "Clap on to that starboard windlass brake, sonny."

Wilbur saw the Chinamen ranging themselves about what he guessed was the windlass in the schooner's bow. He followed and took his place among them, grasping one of the bars.

"Break down!" came the next order. Wilbur and the Chinamen obeyed, bearing up and down upon the bars till the slack of the anchor-chain came home and stretched taut and dripping from the hawse-holes.

Shanghaied

" 'Vast heavin' !"

And then as Wilbur released the brake
and turned about for the next order, he
cast his glance out upon the bay, and
there, not a hundred and fifty yards
away, her spotless sails tense, her cordage
humming, her immaculate flanks slipping
easily through the waves, the water hissing and churning under her forefoot,
clean, gleaming, dainty, and aristocratic,
the Ridgeways' yacht *Petrel* passed like a
thing of life. Wilbur saw Nat Ridgeway
himself at the wheel. Girls in smart
gowns and young fellows in white ducks
and yachting caps—all friends of his—
crowded the decks. A little orchestra of
musicians were reeling off a quickstep.

The popping of a cork and a gale of talk
and laughter came to his ears. Wilbur
stared at the picture, his face devoid of
expression. The *Petrel* came on—drew
nearer—was not a hundred feet away
from the schooner's stern. A strong
swimmer, such as Wilbur, could cover

the distance in a few strokes.   Two minutes ago Wilbur might have——

"Set your mains'l," came the bellow
of Captain Kitchell.   "Clap on to your
throat and peak halyards."

The Chinamen hurried aft.

Wilbur followed.

II

A Nautical Education

In the course of the next few moments, while the little vessel was being got under way, and while the Ridgeways' *Petrel* gleamed off into the blue distance, Wilbur made certain observations.

The name of the boat on which he found himself was the *Bertha Millner*. She was a two-topmast, 28-ton keel schooner, 40 feet long, carrying a large spread of sail—mainsail, foresail, jib, flying-jib, two gaff-topsails, and a staysail. She was very dirty and smelt abominably of some kind of rancid oil. Her crew were Chinamen; there was no mate. But the cook — himself a Chinaman — who appeared from time to time at the door of the galley, a potato-masher in his hand, seemed to have some sort of authority over the hands. He acted in a man-

ner as a go-between for the Captain and
the crew, sometimes interpreting the former's orders, and occasionally giving one
of his own.

Wilbur heard the Captain address him
as Charlie. He spoke pigeon English
fairly. Of the balance of the crew—the
five Chinamen—Wilbur could make nothing. They never spoke, neither to Captain Kitchell, to Charlie, nor to each other;
and for all the notice they took of Wilbur
he might easily have been a sack of sand.
Wilbur felt that his advent on the *Bertha
Millner* was by its very nature an extraordinary event; but the absolute indifference of these brown-suited Mongols, the
blankness of their flat, fat faces, the dul-
ness of their slanting, fishlike eyes that
never met his own or even wandered in
his direction, was uncanny, disquieting.
In what strange venture was he now to
be involved, toward what unknown vor-
tex was this new current setting, this
current that had so suddenly snatched

him from the solid ground of his accustomed life?

He told himself grimly that he was to have a free cruise up the bay, perhaps as far as Alviso; perhaps the *Bertha Millner* would even make the circuit of the bay before returning to San Francisco. He might be gone a week. Wilbur could already see the scare-heads of the daily papers the next morning, chronicling the disappearance of "One of Society's Most Popular Members."

"That's well, y'r throat halyards. Here, Lilee of the Vallee, give a couple of pulls on y'r peak halyard purchase."

Wilbur stared at the Captain helplessly.

"No can tell, hey?" inquired Charlie from the galley. "Pullum disa lope, sabe?"

Wilbur tugged at the rope the cook indicated.

"That's well, y'r peak halyard purchase," chanted Captain Kitchell.

Moran of the Lady Letty

Wilbur made the rope fast. The
mainsail was set, and hung slatting and
flapping in the wind. Next the for'sail
was set in much the same manner, and
Wilbur was ordered to "lay out on the
ji'boom and cast the gaskets off the jib."
He "lay out" as best he could and cast
off the gaskets—he knew barely enough
of yachting to understand an order here
and there—and by the time he was back
on the fo'c'sle head the Chinamen were
at the jib halyard and hoisting away.

"That's well, y'r jib halyards."

The *Bertha Millner* veered round and
played off to the wind, tugging at her
anchor.

"Man y'r windlass."

Wilbur and the crew jumped once
more to the brakes.

"Brake down, heave y'r anchor to the
cathead."

The anchor-chain, already taut, vi-
brated and then cranked through the
hawse-holes as the hands rose and fell at

the brakes. The anchor came home, dripping gray slime. A nor'west wind filled the schooner's sails, a strong ebb tide caught her under-foot.

"We're off," muttered Wilbur, as the *Bertha Millner* heeled to the first gust.

But evidently the schooner was not bound up the bay.

"Must be Vallejo or Benicia, then," hazarded Wilbur, as the sails grew tenser and the water rippled ever louder under the schooner's forefoot. "Maybe they're going after hay or wheat."

The schooner was tacking, headed directly for Meiggs's wharf. She came in closer and closer, so close that Wilbur could hear the talk of the fishermen sitting on the stringpieces. He had just made up his mind that they were to make a landing there, when—

"Stand by for stays," came the raucous bark of the Captain, who had taken the wheel. The sails slatted furiously as the schooner came about. Then the *Bertha*

Millner caught the wind again and lay over quietly and contentedly to her work. The next tack brought the schooner close under Alcatraz. The sea became heavier, the breeze grew stiff and smelt of the outside ocean. Out beyond them to westward opened the Golden Gate, a bleak vista of gray-green water roughened with white-caps.

"Stand by for stays."

Once again, as the rudder went hard over, the *Bertha Millner* fretted and danced and shook her sails, calling impatiently for the wind, chafing at its absence like a child reft of a toy. Then again she scooped the nor'wester in the hollow palms of her tense canvases and settled quietly down on the new tack, her bowsprit pointing straight toward the Presidio.

"We'll come about again soon," Wilbur told himself, "and stand over toward the Contra Costa shore."

A fine huge breath of wind passed

over the schooner. She heeled it on the instant, the water roaring along her quarter, but she kept her course. Wilbur fell thoughtful again, never more keenly observant.

"She must come about soon," he muttered uneasily, "if she's going to stand up toward Vallejo." His heart sank with a sudden apprehension. A nervousness he could not overcome seized upon him. The *Bertha Millner* held tenaciously to the tack. Within fifty yards of the Presidio came the command again:

"Stand by for stays."

Once more, her bows dancing, her cordage rattling, her sails flapping noisily, the schooner came about. Anxiously Wilbur observed the bowsprit as it circled like a hand on a dial, watching where now it would point. It wavered, fluctuated, rose, fell, then settled easily, pointing toward Lime Point. Wilbur felt a sudden coldness at his heart.

"This isn't going to be so much fun,"

he muttered between his teeth. The schooner was not bound up the bay for Alviso nor to Vallejo for grain. The track toward Lime Point could mean but one thing. The wind was freshening from the nor'west, the ebb tide rushing out to meet the ocean like a mill-race, at every moment the Golden Gate opened out wider, and within two minutes after the time of the last tack the *Bertha Millner* heeled to a great gust that had come booming in between the heads, straight from the open Pacific.

"Stand by for stays."

As before, one of the Chinese hands stood by the sail rope of the jib.

"Draw y'r jib."

The jib filled. The schooner came about on the port tack; Lime Point fell away over the stern rail. The huge ground swells began to come in, and as she rose and bowed to the first of these it was precisely as though the *Bertha Millner* were making her courtesy to the great gray ocean, now for the first time in full sight on her starboard quarter.

The schooner was beating out to sea through the Middle Channel. Once clear of the Golden Gate, she stood over toward the Cliff House, then on the next tack cleared Point Bonita. The sea began building up in deadly earnest—they were about to cross the bar. Everything was battened down, the scuppers were awash, and the hawse-holes spouted like fountains after every plunge. Once the Captain ordered all men aloft, just in time to escape a gigantic dull green roller that broke like a Niagara over the schooner's bows, smothering the decks knee-deep in a twinkling.

The wind blew violent and cold, the spray was flying like icy small-shot. Without intermission the *Bertha Millner* rolled and plunged and heaved and sank. Wilbur was drenched to the skin and sore in every joint, from being shunted from rail to mast and from mast to rail again.

Moran of the Lady Letty

The cordage sang like harp-strings, the
schooner's forefoot crushed down into
the heaving water with a hissing like
that of steam, blocks rattled, the Captain
bellowed his orders, rope-ends flogged the
hollow deck till it reverberated like a
drum-head. The crossing of the bar was
one long half-hour of confusion and dis-
cordant sound.

When they were across the bar the
Captain ordered the cook to give the men
their food.

"Git for'rd, sonny," he added, fixing
Wilbur with his eye. "Git for'rd, this
is tawble dee hote, savy?"

Wilbur crawled forward on the reeling
deck, holding on now to a mast, now to
a belaying-pin, now to a stay, watching
his chance and going on between the in-
ebriated plunges of the schooner.

He descended the fo'c'sle hatch. The
Chinamen were already there, sitting
on the edges of their bunks. On the
floor, at the bottom of the ladder, punk-

sticks were burning in an old tomato-
can.

Charlie brought in supper—stewed beef
and pork in a bread-pan and a wooden
kit—and the Chinamen ate it in silence
with their sheath-knives and from tin
plates. A liquid that bore a distant re-
semblance to coffee was served. Wilbur
learned afterward to know the stuff as
Black Jack, and to be aware that it was
made from bud barley and was sweetened
with molasses. A single reeking lamp
swung with the swinging of the schooner
over the centre of the group, and long
afterward Wilbur could remember the
grisly scene—the punk-sticks, the bread-
pan full of hunks of meat, the horrid
close and oily smell, and the circle of
silent, preoccupied Chinese, each sitting
on his bunk-ledge, devouring stewed pork
and holding his pannikin of Black Jack
between his feet against the rolling of the
boat.

Wilbur looked fearfully at the mess

in the pan, recalling the chocolate and stuffed olives that had been his last luncheon.

"Well," he muttered, clenching his teeth, "I've got to come to it sooner or later." His penknife was in the pocket of his waistcoat, underneath his oilskin coat. He opened the big blade, harpooned a cube of pork, and deposited it on his tin plate. He ate it slowly and with savage determination. But the Black Jack was more than he could bear.

"I'm not hungry enough for that just now," he told himself. "Say, Jim," he said, turning to the Chinaman next him on the bunk-ledge, "say, what kind of boat is this? What you do—where you go?"

The other moved away impatiently.

"No sabe, no sabe," he answered, shaking his head and frowning. Throughout the whole of that strange meal these were the only words spoken.

A Nautical Education

When Wilbur came on deck again he noted that the *Bertha Millner* had already left the whistling-buoy astern. Off to the east, her sails just showing above the waves, was a pilot-boat with the number 7 on her mainsail. The evening was closing in; the Farallones were in plain sight dead ahead. Far behind, in a mass of shadow just bluer than the sky, he could make out a few twinkling lights—San Francisco.

Half an hour later Kitchell came on deck from his supper in cabin aft. He glanced in the direction of the mainland, now almost out of sight, then took the wheel from one of the Chinamen and commanded, "Ease off y'r fore an' main sheets." The hands eased away and the schooner played off before the wind.

The staysail was set. The *Bertha Millner* headed to southwest, bowing easily ahead of a good eight-knot breeze.

Next came the order "All hands aft!" and Wilbur and his mates betook themselves to the quarterdeck. Charlie took the wheel, and he and Kitchell began to choose the men for their watches, just as Wilbur remembered to have chosen sides for baseball during his school days.

"Sonny, I'll choose you; you're on my watch," said the Captain to Wilbur, "and I will assoom the ree-sponsibility of you nautical eddoocation."

"I may as well tell you at once," began Wilbur, "that I'm no sailor."

"But you will be, soon," answered the Captain, at once soothing and threatening; "you will be, Mister Lilee of the Vallee, you kin lay to it, as how you will be one of the best sailor men along the front, as our dear friend Jim says. Before I git thoo with you, you'll be a sailor man or shark-bait, I can promise you. You're on my watch; step over here, son."

The watches were divided, Charlie and three other Chinamen on the port, Kitchell, Wilbur, and two Chinamen on the

starboard. The men trooped forward
again.

The tiny world of the schooner had
lapsed to quiet. The *Bertha Millner* was
now clear of the land, that lay like a blur
of faintest purple smoke—ever growing
fainter—low in the east. The Farallones showed but their shoulders above
the horizon. The schooner was standing
well out from shore—even beyond the
track of the coasters and passenger
steamers—to catch the trades from the
northwest. The sun was setting royally,
and the floor of the ocean shimmered like
mosaic. The sea had gone down and the
fury of the bar was a thing forgotten. It
was perceptibly warmer.

On board, the two watches mingled forward, smoking opium and playing a game
that looked like checkers. Three of them
were washing down the decks with kaiar
brooms. For the first time since he had
come on board Wilbur heard the sound
of their voices.

Moran of the Lady Letty

The evening was magnificent. Never to Wilbur's eyes had the Pacific appeared so vast, so radiant, so divinely beautiful. A star or two burnt slowly through that part of the sky where the pink began to fade into the blue. Charlie went forward and set the side lights—red on the port rigging, green on the starboard. As he passed Wilbur, who was leaning over the rail and watching the phosphorus flashing just under the surface, he said:

"Hey, you go talkee-talk one-piecey Boss, savvy Boss—chin-chin."

Wilbur went aft and came up on the poop, where Kitchell stood at the wheel, smoking an inverted "Tarrier's Delight."

"Now, son," began Kitchell, "I natch'ly love you so that I'm goin' to do you a reel favor, do you twig? I'm goin' to allow you to berth aft in the cabin, 'long o' me an' Charlie, an' beesides you can make free of my quarterdeck. Mebbee you ain't used to the ways of sailor men just yet, but you can lay it to

that those two are reel concessions, savvy?
I ain't a mush-head, like mee dear friend
Jim. You ain't no water-front swine, I
can guess that with one hand tied bee-
hind me. You're a toff, that's what you
are, and your lines has been laid for toffs.
I ain't askin' you no questions, but you
got brains, an' I figger on gettin' more
outa you by lettin' you have y'r head a
bit. But mind, now, you get gay once,
sonny, or try to flimflam me, or forget
that I'm the boss of the bathtub, an'
strike me blind, I'll cut you open, an' you
can lay to that, son. Now, then, here's
the game: You work this boat 'long with
the coolies, an' take my orders, an' walk
chalk, an' I'll teach you navigation,
an' make this cruise as easy as how-
do-you-do. You don't, an' I'll man-
handle you till y'r bones come throo y'r
hide."

"I've no choice in the matter," said
Wilbur. "I've got to make the best of a
bad situation."

Moran of the Lady Letty

"I ree-marked as how you had brains," muttered the Captain.

"But there's one thing," continued Wilbur; "if I'm to have my head a little, as you say, you'll find we can get along better if you put me to rights about this whole business. Why was I brought aboard, why are there only Chinese along, where are we going, what are we going to do, and how long are we going to be gone?"

Kitchell spat over the side, and then sucked the nicotine from his mustache.

"Well," he said, resuming his pipe, "it's like this, son. This ship belongs to one of the Six Chinese Companies of Chinatown in Frisco. Charlie, here, is one of the shareholders in the business. We go down here twice a year off Cape Sain' Lucas, Lower California, an' fish for blue sharks, or white, if we kin ketch 'em. We get the livers of these an' try out the oil, an' we bring back that same oil, an' the Chinamen sell it all over San

A Nautical Education

Francisco as simon-pure cod-liver oil,
savvy? An' it pays like a nitrate bed.
I come in because it's a Custom-House
regulation that no coolie can take a boat
out of Frisco."

"And how do I come in?" asked Wilbur.

"Mee dear friend Jim put a knock-me-
out drop into your Manhattan cocktail.
It's a capsule filled with a drug. You
were shanghaied, son," said the Captain,
blandly.

.   .   .   .   .

About an hour later Wilbur turned in.
Kitchell showed him his bunk with its
"donkey's breakfast" and single ill-smell-
ing blanket. It was located under the
companion-way that led down into the
cabin. Kitchell bunked on one side,
Charlie on the other. A hacked deal
table, covered with oilcloth and ironed to
the floor, a swinging-lamp, two chairs, a
rack of books, a chest or two, and a flar-
ing picture cut from the advertisement of

a ballet, was the room's inventory in the matter of furniture and ornament.

Wilbur sat on the edge of his bunk before undressing, reviewing the extraordinary events of the day. In a moment he was aware of a movement in one of the other two bunks, and presently made out Charlie lying on his side and holding in the flame of an alcohol lamp a skewer on which some brown and sticky stuff boiled and sizzled. He transferred the stuff to the bowl of a huge pipe and drew on it noisily once or twice. In another moment he had sunk back in his bunk, nearly senseless, but with a long breath of an almost blissful contentment.

"Beast!" muttered Wilbur, with profound disgust.

He threw off his oilskin coat and felt in the pocket of his waistcoat (which he had retained when he had changed his clothes in the fo'c'stle) for his watch. He drew it out. It was just nine o'clock. All at once an idea occurred to him. He fumbled in another pocket of the waistcoat and brought out one of his calling-cards.

For a moment Wilbur remained motionless, seated on the bunk-ledge, smiling grimly, while his glance wandered now to the sordid cabin of the *Bertha Millner* and the opium-drugged coolie sprawled on the "donkey's breakfast," and now to the card in his hand on which a few hours ago he had written:

"First waltz—Jo."

III

The Lady Letty

ANOTHER day passed, then two. Before Wilbur knew it he had settled himself to his new life, and woke one morning to the realization that he was positively enjoying himself. Daily the weather grew warmer. The fifth day out from San Francisco it was actually hot. The pitch grew soft in the *Bertha Millner's* deck seams, the masts sweated resin. The Chinamen went about the decks wearing but their jeans and blouses. Kitchell had long since abandoned his coat and vest. Wilbur's oilskins became intolerable, and he was at last constrained to trade his pocket-knife to Charlie for a suit of jeans and wicker sandals, such as the coolies wore—and odd enough he looked in them.

The Captain instructed him in steering, and even promised to show him the use of the sextant and how to take an observation in the fake short and easy coasting style of navigation. Furthermore, he showed him how to read the log and the manner of keeping the dead reckoning.

During most of his watches Wilbur was engaged in painting the inside of the cabin, door panels, lintels, and the few scattered mouldings; and toward the middle of the first week out, when the *Bertha Millner* was in the latitude of Point Conception, he and three Chinamen, under Kitchell's direction, ratlined down the forerigging and affixed the crow's nest upon the for'mast. The next morning, during Charlie's watch on deck, a Chinaman was sent up into the crow's nest, and from that time on there was always a lookout maintained from the masthead.

Moran of the Lady Letty

More than once Wilbur looked around him at the empty coruscating indigo of the ocean floor, wondering at the necessity of the lookout, and finally expressed his curiosity to Kitchell. The Captain had by now taken not a little to Wilbur; at first for the sake of a white man's company, and afterward because he began to place a certain vague reliance upon Wilbur's judgment. Kitchell had reemarked as how he had brains.

"Well, you see, son," Kitchell had explained to Wilbur, "os-tensiblee we are after shark-liver oil—and so we are; but also we are on any lay that turns up; ready for any game, from wrecking to barratry. Strike me, if I haven't thought of scuttling the dough-dish for her insoorance. There's regular trade, son, to be done in ships, and then there's pickin's an' pickin's, an' pickin's. Lord, the ocean's rich with pickin's. Do you know there's millions made out of the day-bree and refuse of a big city?

The Lady Letty

How about an ocean's day-bree, just chew on that notion a turn; an' as fur a lookout, lemmee tell you, son, cast your eye out yon," and he swept the sea with a forearm; "nothin', hey, so it looks, but lemmee tell you, son, there ain't no manner of place on the ball of dirt where you're likely to run up afoul of so many things—unexpected things—as at sea. When you're clear o' land lay to this here pree-cep', 'A million to one on the unexpected.'"

The next day fell almost dead calm. The hale, lusty-lunged nor'wester that had snorted them forth from the Golden Gate had lapsed to a zephyr, the schooner rolled lazily southward with the leisurely nonchalance of a grazing ox. At noon, just after dinner, a few cat's-paws curdled the milky-blue whiteness of the glassy surface, and the water once more began to talk beneath the bowsprit. It was very hot. The sun spun silently like a spinning brass discus over the mainmast.

Moran of the Lady Letty

On the fo'c's'le head the Chinamen were asleep or smoking opium. It was Charlie's watch. Kitchell dozed in his hammock in the shadow of the main-sheet. Wilbur was below tinkering with his paint-pot about the cabin. The stillness was profound. It was the stillness of the summer sea at high noon.

The lookout in the crow's nest broke the quiet.

"Hy-yah, hy-yah!" he cried, leaning from the barrel and calling through an arched palm. "Hy-yah, one, two, plenty, many tortle, topside wattah; hy-yah, all-same tortle."

"Hello, hello!" cried the Captain, rolling from his hammock. "Turtle? Where-away?"

"I tink-um 'bout quallah mile, meb-bee, four-piecee tortle all-same weatha bow."

"Turtle, hey? Down y'r wheel, Jim, haul y'r jib to win'ward," he commanded the man at the wheel; then to the men forward: "Get the dory overboard. Son, Charlie, and you, Wing, tumble in. Wake up now and see you stay so."

The dory was swung over the side, and the men dropped into her and took their places at the oars. "Give way," cried the Captain, settling himself in the bow with the gaff in his hand. "Hey, Jim!" he shouted to the lookout far above, "hey, lay our course for us." The lookout nodded, the oars fell, and the dory shot forward in the direction indicated by the lookout.

"Kin you row, son?" asked Kitchell, with sudden suspicion. Wilbur smiled.

"You ask Charlie and Wing to ship their oars and give me a pair." The Captain complied, hesitating.

"Now, what," he said grimly, "now, what do you think you're going to do, sonny?"

"I'm going to show you the Bob Cook stroke we used in our boat in '95, when we beat Harvard," answered Wilbur.

Kitchell gazed doubtfully at the first
few strokes, then with growing interest
watched the tremendous reach, the powerful knee-drive, the swing, the easy
catch, and the perfect recover. The dory
was cutting the water like a gasoline
launch, and between strokes there was
the least possible diminishing of the
speed.

"I'm a bit out of form just now," remarked Wilbur, "and I'm used to the
sliding seat; but I guess it'll do." Kitchell glanced at the human machine that
once was No. 5 in the Yale boat and then
at the water hissing from the dory's
bows. "My Gawd!" he said, under his
breath. He spat over the bows and
sucked the nicotine from his mustache,
thoughtfully.

"I ree-marked," he observed, "as how
you had brains, my son."

A few minutes later the Captain, who
was standing in the dory's bow and alter-
nately conning the ocean's surface and

looking back to the Chinaman standing on the schooner's masthead, uttered an exclamation:

"Steady, ship your oars, quiet now, quiet, you damn fools! We're right on 'em—four, by Gawd, an' big as dinin'-tables!"

The oars were shipped. The dory's speed dwindled. "Out your paddles, sit on the gun'l, and paddle ee-asy." The hands obeyed. The Captain's voice dropped to a whisper. His back was toward them and he gestured with one free hand. Looking out over the water from his seat on the gun'l, Wilbur could make out a round, greenish mass like a patch of floating seaweed, just under the surface, some sixty yards ahead.

"Easy sta'board," whispered the Captain under his elbow. "Go ahead, port; e-e-easy all, steady, steady."

The affair began to assume the intensity of a little drama—a little drama of midocean. In spite of himself, Wilbur was excited. He even found occasion to observe that the life was not so bad, after all. This was as good fun as stalking deer. The dory moved forward by inches. Kitchell's whisper was as faint as a dying infant's: "Steady all, s-stead-ee, sh-stead——"

He lunged forward sharply with the gaff, and shouted aloud: "I got him—grab holt his tail flippers, you fool swabs; grab holt quick—don't you leggo—got him there, Charlie? If he gets away, you swine, I'll rip y' open with the gaff — heave now—heave—there—there — soh, stand clear his nippers. Strike me! he's a whacker. I thought he was going to get away. Saw me just as I swung the gaff, an' ducked his nut."

Over the side, bundled without cere-mony into the boat, clawing, thrashing, clattering, and blowing like the exhaust of a donkey-engine, tumbled the great green turtle, his wet, green shield of shell three feet from edge to edge, the gaff firmly transfixed in his body, just under the fore-flipper. From under his shell protruded his snake-like head and neck, withered like that of an old man. He was waving his head from side to side, the jaws snapping like a snapped silk handkerchief. Kitchell thrust him away with a paddle. The turtle craned his neck, and, catching the bit of wood in his jaw, bit it in two in a single grip.

"I tol' you so, I tol' you to stand clear his snapper. If that had been your shin now, eh? Hello, what's that?"

Faintly across the water came a prolonged hallooing from the schooner. Kitchell stood up in the dory, shading his eyes with his hat.

"What's biting 'em now?" he muttered, with the uneasiness of a captain away from his ship. "Oughta left Charlie on board—or you, son. Who's doin' that yellin', I can't make out."

"Up in the crow's nest," exclaimed Wilbur. "It's Jim, see, he's waving his arms."

"Well, whaduz he wave his dam' fool arms for?" growled Kitchell, angry because something was going forward he did not understand.

"There, he's shouting again. Listen— I can't make out what he's yelling."

"He'll yell to a different pipe when I get my grip of him. I'll twist the head of that swab till he'll have to walk back'ard to see where he's goin'. Whaduz he wave his arms for—whaduz he yell like a dam' philly-loo bird for? What's him say, Charlie?"

"Jim heap sing, no can tell. Mebbee — tinkum sing, come back chopchop."

"We'll see. Oars out, men, give way. Now, son, put a little o' that Yale stingo in the stroke."

In the crow's nest Jim still yelled and waved like one distraught, while the dory returned at a smart clip toward the schooner. Kitchell lathered with fury.

"Oh-h," he murmured softly through

his gritted teeth. "Jess lemmee lay mee two hands afoul of you wunst, you gibbering, yellow philly-loo bird, believe me, you'll dance. Shut up!" he roared; "shut up, you crazy do-do, ain't we coming fast as we can?"

The dory bumped alongside, and the Captain was over the rail like quicksilver. The hands were all in the bow, looking and pointing to the west. Jim slid down the ratlines, bubbling over with suppressed news. Before his feet had touched the deck Kitchell had kicked him into the stays again, fulminating blasphemies.

"Sing!" he shouted, as the Chinaman clambered away like a bewildered ape; "sing a little more. I would if I were you. Why don't you sing and wave, you dam' fool philly-loo bird?"

"Yas, sah," answered the coolie.

"What you yell for? Charlie, ask him whaffo him sing."

"I tink-um ship," answered Charlie

calmly, looking out over the starboard quarter.

"Ship!"

"Him velly sick," hazarded the China-man from the ratlines, adding a sentence in Chinese to Charlie.

"He says he tink-um ship sick, all same; ask um something—ship velly sick."

By this time the Captain, Wilbur, and all on board could plainly make out a sail some eight miles off the starboard bow. Even at that distance, and to eyes so inexperienced as those of Wilbur, it needed but a glance to know that some-thing was wrong with her. It was not that she failed to ride the waves with even keel, it was not that her rigging was in disarray, nor that her sails were disor-dered. Her distance was too great to make out such details. But in precisely the same manner as a trained physician glances at a doomed patient, and from that indefinable look in the face of him

and the eyes of him pronounces the ver-
dict "death," so Kitchell took in the
stranger with a single comprehensive
glance, and exclaimed:

"Wreck!"

"Yas, sah. I tink-um velly sick."

"Oh, go to 'll, or go below and fetch
up my glass—hustle!"

The glass was brought. "Son," exclaimed Kitchell—"where is that man
with the brains? Son, come aloft here
with me." The two clambered up the
ratlines to the crow's nest. Kitchell adjusted the glass.

"She's a bark," he muttered, "iron
built—about seven hundred tons, I
guess—in distress. There's her ensign
upside down at the mizz'nhead—looks
like Norway—an' her distress signals on
the spanker gaff. Take a blink at her,
son—what do you make her out? Lord,
she's ridin' high."

Wilbur took the glass, catching the
stranger after several clumsy attempts.

She was, as Captain Kitchell had announced, a bark, and, to judge by her flag, evidently Norwegian.

"How she rolls!" muttered Wilbur.

"That's what I can't make out," answered Kitchell. "A bark such as she ain't ought to roll thata way; her ballast'd steady her."

"What's the flags on that boom aft— one's red and white and square-shaped, and the other's the same color, only swallow-tail in shape?"

"That's H. B., meanin': 'I am in need of assistance.'"

"Well, where's the crew? I don't see anybody on board."

"Oh, they're there right enough."

"Then they're pretty well concealed about the premises," returned Wilbur, as he passed the glass to the Captain.

"She does seem kinda empty," said the Captain in a moment, with a sudden show of interest that Wilbur failed to understand.

The Lady Letty

"An' where's her boats?" continued Kitchell. "I don't just quite make out any boats at all." There was a long silence.

"Seems to be a sort of haze over her," observed Wilbur.

"I noticed that, air kinda quivers oily-like. No boats, no boats—an' I can't see anybody aboard." Suddenly Kitchell lowered the glass and turned to Wilbur. He was a different man. There was a new shine in his eyes, a wicked line appeared over the nose, the jaw grew salient, prognathous.

"Son," he exclaimed, gimleting Wilbur with his contracted eyes; "I have reemarked as how you had brains. I kin fool the coolies, but I can't fool you. It looks to me as if that bark yonder was a derelict; an' do you know what that means to us? Chaw on it a turn."

"A derelict?"

"If there's a crew on board they're concealed from the public gaze — an' where are the boats then? I figger she's an abandoned derelict. Do you know what that means for us—for you and I? It means," and gripping Wilbur by the shoulders, he spoke the word into his face with a savage intensity. "It means salvage, do you savvy?—salvage, salvage. Do you figger what salvage on a seven-hundred-tonner would come to? Well, just lemmee drop it into your think tank, an' lay to what I say. It's all the ways from fifty to seventy thousand dollars, whatever her cargo is; call it sixty thousand—thirty thou' apiece. Oh, I don't know!" he exclaimed, lapsing to landman's slang. "Wha'd I say about a million to one on the unexpected at sea?"

"Thirty thousand!" exclaimed Wilbur, without thought as yet.

"Now y'r singin' songs," cried the Captain. "Listen to me, son," he went on, rapidly shutting up the glass and thrusting it back in the case; "my name's Kitchell, and I'm hog right through."

The Lady Letty

He emphasized the words with a levelled forefinger, his eyes flashing. H—O—G spells very truly yours, Alvinza Kitchell —ninety-nine swine an' me make a hundred swine. I'm a shoat with both feet in the trough, first, last, an' always. If that bark's abandoned, an' I says she is, she's ours. I'm out for anything that there's stuff in. I guess I'm more of a beach-comber by nature than anything else. If she's abandoned she belongs to us. To 'll with this coolie game. We'll go beach-combin', you an' I. We'll board that bark and work her into the nearest port—San Diego, I guess—and get the salvage on her if we have to swim in her. Are you with me?" he held out his hand. The man was positively trembling from head to heel. It was impossible to resist the excitement of the situation, its novelty—the high crow's nest of the schooner, the keen salt air, the Chinamen grouped far below, the indigo of the warm ocean, and out yonder the forsaken derelict, rolling her light hull till the garboard streak flashed in the sun.

"Well, of course, I'm with you, Cap," exclaimed Wilbur, gripping Kitchell's hand. "When there's thirty thousand to be had for the asking I guess I'm a 'na'chel bawn' beach-comber myself."

"Now, nothing about this to the coolies."

"But how will you make out with your owners, the Six Companies? Aren't you bound to bring the *Bertha* in?"

"Rot my owners!" exclaimed Kitchell. "I ain't a skipper of no oil-boat any longer. I'm a beach-comber." He fixed the wallowing bark with glistening eyes. "Gawd strike me," he murmured, "ain'r she a daisy? It's a little Klondike. Come on, son."

The two went down the ratlines, and Kitchell ordered a couple of the hands into the dory that had been rowing astern. He and Wilbur followed. Charlie was left on board, with direction to lay the schooner to. The dory flew over the water, Wilbur setting the stroke. In a few moments she was well up with the bark. Though a larger boat than the *Bertha Millner*, she was rolling in lamentable fashion, and every laboring heave showed her bottom encrusted with barnacles and seaweed.

Her fore and main tops'ls and to'gallants'ls were set, as also were her lower stays'ls and royals. But the braces seemed to have parted, and the yards were swinging back and forth in their ties. The spanker was brailed up, and the spanker boom thrashed idly over the poop as the bark rolled and rolled and rolled. The mainmast was working in its shoe, the rigging and backstays sagged. An air of abandonment, of unspeakable loneliness, of abomination hung about her. Never had Wilbur seen anything more utterly alone. Within three lengths the Captain rose in his place and shouted:

"Bark ahoy!" There was no answer.

Moran of the Lady Letty

Thrice he repeated the call, and thrice
the dismal thrashing of the spanker boom
and the flapping of the sails was the only
answer. Kitchell turned to Wilbur in
triumph. "I guess she's ours," he whispered. They were now close enough to
make out the bark's name upon her
counter. *Lady Letty*, and Wilbur was
in the act of reading it aloud, when a
huge brown dorsal fin, like the triangular
sail of a lugger, cut the water between
the dory and the bark.

"Shark!" said Kitchell; "and there's
another!" he exclaimed in the next instant, "and another! Strike me, the
water's alive with 'em! There's a stiff
on the bark, you can lay to that"; and at
that, acting on some strange impulse, he
called again, "Bark ahoy!" There was
no response.

The dory was now well up to the derelict, and pretty soon a prolonged and vi-
bratory hissing noise, strident, insistent,
smote upon their ears.

The Lady Letty

"What's that?" exclaimed Wilbur, perplexed. The Captain shook his head, and just then, as the bark rolled almost to her scuppers in their direction, a glimpse of the deck was presented to their view. It was only a glimpse, gone on the instant, as the bark rolled back to port, but it was time enough for Wilbur and the Captain to note the parted and open seams and the deck bulging, and in one corner blown up and splintered.

The Captain smote a thigh.

"Coal!" he cried. "Anthracite coal. The coal he't up and generated gas, of course—no fire, y'understand, just gas— gas blew up the deck—no way of stopping combustion. Naturally they had to cut for it. Smell the gas, can't you! No wonder she's hissing—no wonder she rolled—cargo goes off in gas—and what's to weigh her down? I was wondering what could 'a wrecked her in this weather. Lord, it's as plain as Billy-b'damn."

The dory was alongside. Kitchell

watched his chance, and as the bark
rolled down caught the mainyard-brace
hanging in a bight over the rail and
swung himself to the deck. "Look
sharp!" he called, as Wilbur followed.
"It won't do for you to fall among them
shark, son. Just look at the hundreds
of 'em. There's a stiff on board, sure."

Wilbur steadied himself on the sway-
ing broken deck, choking against the reek
of coal-gas that hissed upward on every
hand. The heat was almost like a fur-
nace. Everything metal was intolerable
to the touch.

"She's abandoned, sure," muttered the
captain. "Look," and he pointed to the
empty chocks on the house and the
severed lashings. "Oh, it's a haul, son;
it's a haul, an' you can lay to that.
Now, then, cabin first," and he started
aft.

But it was impossible to go into the
cabin. The moment the door was opened
suffocating billows of gas rushed out and

beat them back. On the third trial the Captain staggered out, almost overcome with its volume.

"Can't get in there for a while yet," he gasped, "but I saw the stiff on the floor by the table; looks like the old man. He's spit his false teeth out. I knew there was a stiff aboard."

"Then there's more than one," said Wilbur. "See there!" From behind the wheel-box in the stern protruded a hand and forearm in an oilskin sleeve.

Wilbur ran up, peered over the little space between the wheel and the wheel-box, and looked straight into a pair of eyes—eyes that were alive. Kitchell came up.

"One left, anyhow," he muttered, looking over Wilbur's shoulder; "sailor man, though; can't interfere with our salvage. The bark's derelict, right enough. Shake him out of there, son; can't you see, the lad's dotty with the gas?"

Cramped into the narrow space of the

wheel-box like a terrified hare in a blind
burrow was the figure of a young boy.
So firmly was he wedged into the corner
that Kitchell had to kick down the box
before he could be reached. The boy
spoke no word. Stupefied with the gas,
he watched them with vacant eyes.

Wilbur put a hand under the lad's arm
and got him to his feet. He was a tall,
well-made fellow, with ruddy complexion
and milk-blue eyes, and was dressed, as
if for heavy weather, in oilskins.

"Well, sonny, you've had a fine mess
aboard here," said Kitchell. The boy—
he might have been two and twenty—
stared and frowned.

"Clean loco from the gas. Get him
into the dory, son. I'll try this bloody
cabin again."

Kitchell turned back and descended
from the poop, and Wilbur, his arm
around the boy, followed. Kitchell was
already out of hearing, and Wilbur was
bracing himself upon the rolling deck,

steadying the young fellow at his side, when the latter heaved a deep breath. His throat and breast swelled. Wilbur stared sharply, with a muttered exclamation:

"My God, it's a girl!" he said.

IV

Moran

MEANWHILE Charlie had brought the *Bertha Millner* up to within hailing distance of the bark, and had hove her to. Kitchell ordered Wilbur to return to the schooner and bring over a couple of axes.

" We'll have to knock holes all through the house, and break in the skylights, and let the gas escape before we can do anything. Take the kid over and give him whiskey ; then come along back and bear a hand."

Wilbur had considerable difficulty in getting into the dory from the deck of the plunging derelict with his dazed and almost helpless charge. Even as he slid down the rope into the little boat and helped the girl to follow, he was aware of two dull, brownish-green shadows moving just beneath the water's surface not ten feet away, and knew that he was being stealthily watched. The Chinamen at the oars of the dory, with that extraordinary absence of curiosity which is the mark of the race, did not glance a second time at the survivor of the *Lady Letty's* misadventure. To them it was evident she was but a for'mast hand. However, Wilbur examined her with extraordinary interest as she sat in the stern sheets, sullen, half-defiant, half-bewildered, and bereft of speech.

She was not pretty—she was too tall for that—quite as tall as Wilbur himself, and her skeleton was too massive. Her face was red, and the glint of blue ice was in her eyes. Her eyelashes and eyebrows, as well as the almost imperceptible down that edged her cheek when she turned against the light, were blonde almost to whiteness. What beauty she had was of the fine, hardy Norse type.

Her hands were red and hard, and even beneath the coarse sleeve of the oilskin coat one could infer that the biceps and deltoids were large and powerful. She was coarse-fibred, no doubt, mentally as well as physically, but her coarseness, so Wilbur guessed, would prove to be the coarseness of a primitive rather than of a degenerate character.

One thing he saw clearly during the few moments of the dory's trip between bark and schooner—the fact that his charge was a woman must be kept from Captain Kitchell. Wilbur knew his man by now. It could be done. Kitchell and he would take the *Lady Letty* into the nearest port as soon as possible. The deception would have to be maintained only for a day or two.

He left the girl on board the schooner and returned to the derelict with the axes. He found Kitchell on the house, just returned from a hasty survey of the prize.

"She's a daisy," vociferated the Captain, as Wilbur came aboard. "I've been havin' a look 'round. She's brand-new. See the date on the capst'n-head? Christiania is her hailin' port—built there; but it's her papers I'm after. Then we'll know where we're at. How's the kid?"

"She's all right," answered Wilbur, before he could collect his thoughts. But the Captain thought he had reference to the *Bertha*.

"I mean the kid we found in the wheel-box. He doesn't count in our salvage. The bark's been abandoned as plain as paint. If I thought he stood in our way," and Kitchell's jaw grew salient, "I'd shut him in the cabin with the old man a spell, till he'd copped off. Now then, son, first thing to do is to chop vents in this yere house."

"Hold up—we can do better than that," said Wilbur, restraining Kitchell's fury of impatience. "Slide the big skylight off—it's loose already."

Moran of the Lady Letty

A couple of the schooner's hands were
ordered aboard the *Lady Letty*, and the
skylight removed. At first the pour of
gas was terrific, but by degrees it abated,
and at the end of half an hour Kitchell
could keep back no longer.

"Come on!" he cried, catching up an
axe; "rot the difference." All the plundering instincts of the man were aroused
and clamoring. He had become a very
wolf within scent of its prey—a veritable
hyena nuzzling about its carrion.

"Lord!" he gasped, "t' think that
everything we see, everything we find, is
ours!"

Wilbur himself was not far behind him
in eagerness. Somewhere deep down in
the heart of every Anglo-Saxon lies the
predatory instinct of his Viking ancestors
—an instinct that a thousand years of re-
spectability and tax-paying have not quite
succeeded in eliminating.

A flight of six steps, brass bound and
bearing the double L of the bark's mono-

gram, led them down into a sort of vestibule. From the vestibule a door opened directly into the main cabin. They entered.

The cabin was some twenty feet long and unusually spacious. Fresh from his recollection of the grime and reek of the schooner, it struck Wilbur as particularly dainty. It was painted white with stripes of blue, gold, and pea-green. On either side three doors opened off into staterooms and private cabins, and with each roll of the derelict these doors banged like an irregular discharge of revolvers. In the centre was the dining-table, covered with a red cloth, very much awry. On each side of the table were four arm-chairs, screwed to the deck, one somewhat larger at the head. Overhead, in swinging-racks, were glasses and decanters of whiskey and some kind of white wine. But for one feature the sight of the *Letty's* cabin was charming. However, on the floor by the sliding-door in the forward bulkhead lay a body, face upward.

The body was that of a middle-aged, fine-looking man, his head covered with the fur, ear-lapped cap that Norwegians affect, even in the tropics. The eyes were wide open, the face discolored. In the last gasp of suffocation the set of false teeth had been forced half-way out of his mouth, distorting the countenance with a hideous simian grin. Instantly Kitchell's eye was caught by the glint of the gold in which these teeth were set.

"Here's about $100 to begin with," he exclaimed, and picking up the teeth, dropped them into his pocket with a wink at Wilbur. The body of the dead Captain was passed up through the skylight and laid out on the deck, and Wilbur and Kitchell turned their attention to what had been his stateroom.

The Captain's room was the largest one of the six staterooms opening from the main cabin.

"Here we are!" exclaimed Kitchell as he and Wilbur entered. "The old man's room, and no mistake."

Besides the bunk, the stateroom was fitted up with a lounge of red plush screwed to the bulkhead. A roll of charts leaned in one corner, an alarm clock, stopped at 1:15, stood on a shelf in the company of some dozen paper-covered novels and a drinking-glass full of cigars. Over the lounge, however, was the rack of instruments, sextant, barometer, chronometer, glass, and the like, securely screwed down, while against the wall, in front of a swivel leather chair that was ironed to the deck, was the locked secretary.

"Look at 'em, just look at 'em, will you!" said Kitchell, running his fingers lovingly over the polished brass of the instruments. "There's a thousand dollars of stuff right here. The chronometer's worth five hundred alone, Bennett

& Sons' own make." He turned to the secretary.

"Now!" he exclaimed with a long breath.

What followed thrilled Wilbur with alternate excitement, curiosity, and a vivid sense of desecration and sacrilege. For the life of him he could not make the thing seem right or legal in his eyes, and yet he had neither the wish nor the power to stay his hand or interfere with what Kitchell was doing.

The Captain put the blade of the axe in the chink of the secretary's door and wrenched it free. It opened down to form a sort of desk, and disclosed an array of cubby-holes and two small doors, both locked. These latter Kitchell smashed in with the axe-head. Then he seated himself in the swivel chair and began to rifle their contents systematically, Wilbur leaning over his shoulder.

The heat from the coal below them was almost unbearable. In the cabin the six doors kept up a continuous ear-shocking fusillade, as though half a dozen men were fighting with revolvers; from without, down the open skylight, came the sing-song talk of the Chinamen and the wash and ripple of the two vessels, now side by side. The air, foul beyond expression, tasted of brass, their heads swam and ached to bursting, but absorbed in their work they had no thought of the lapse of time nor the discomfort of their surroundings. Twice during the examination of the bark's papers, Kitchell sent Wilbur out into the cabin for the whiskey decanter in the swinging-racks.

"Here's the charter papers," said Kitchell, unfolding and spreading them out one by one; "and here's the clearing papers from Blyth in England. This yere's the insoorance, and here, this is— rot that, nothin' but the articles for the crew—no use to us."

In a separate envelope, carefully sealed and bound, they came upon the Captain's

private papers. A marriage certificate
setting forth the union between Eilert
Sternersen, of Fruholmen, Norway, and
Sarah Moran, of some seaport town (the
name was undecipherable) of the North
of England. Next came a birth certificate of a daughter named Moran, dated
twenty-two years back, and a bill of sale
of the bark *Lady Letty*, whereby a two-
thirds interest was conveyed from the
previous owners (a shipbuilding firm of
Christiania) to Capt. Eilert Sternersen.

"The old man was his own boss," commented Kitchell. "Hello!" he remarked,
"look here"; a yellowed photograph was
in his hand, the picture of a stout, fair-
haired woman of about 40, wearing
enormous pendant earrings in the style of
the early sixties. Below was written:
"S. Moran Sternersen, ob. 1867."

"Old woman copped off," said Kitchell, "so much the better for us; no heirs
to put in their gab; an'—hold hard—
steady all—here's the will, s'help me."

Moran

The only items of importance in the will were the confirmation of the wife's death and the expressly stated bequest of "the bark known as, and sailing under, the name of the *Lady Letty* to my only and beloved daughter, Moran."

"Well," said Wilbur.

The Captain sucked his mustache, then furiously, striking the desk with his fist:

"The bark's ours!" there was a certain ring of defiance in his voice. "Damn the will! I ain't so cock-sure about the law, but I'll make sure."

"As how?" said Wilbur.

Kitchell slung the will out of the open port into the sea.

"That's how," he remarked. "I'm the heir. I found the bark; mine she is, an' mine she stays—yours an' mine, that is."

But Wilbur had not even the time to thoroughly enjoy the satisfaction that the Captain's words conveyed, before an idea suddenly presented itself to him. The girl he had found on board of the bark, the ruddy, fair-haired girl of the fine and hardy Norse type. That was the daughter, of course; that was "Moran." Instantly the situation adjusted itself in his imagination. The two inseparables, father and daughter, sailors both, their lives passed together on shipboard, and the *Lady Letty* their dream, their ambition, a vessel that at last they could call their own.

Then this disastrous voyage—perhaps the first in their new craft—the combustion in the coal—the panic terror of the crew and their desertion of the bark, and the sturdy resolution of the father and daughter to bring the *Letty* in—to work her into port alone. They had failed; the father had died from gas; the girl, at least for the moment, was crazed from its effects. But the bark had not been abandoned. The owner was on board. Kitchell was wrong; she was no derelict; not one penny could they gain by her salvage.

Moran

For an instant a wave of bitterest disappointment passed over Wilbur as he saw his $30,000 dwindling to nothing. Then the instincts of habit reasserted themselves. The taxpayer in him was stronger than the freebooter, after all. He felt that it was his duty to see to it that the girl had her rights. Kitchell must be made aware of the situation— must be told that Moran, the daughter, the Captain's heir, was on board the schooner; that the "kid" found in the wheel-box was a girl. But on second thoughts that would never do. Above all things, the brute Kitchell must not be shown that a girl was aboard the schooner on which he had absolute command, nor, setting the question of Moran's sex aside, must Kitchell know her even as the dead Captain's heir. There was a difference in the men here, and Wilbur appreciated it. Kitchell, the law-abiding taxpayer, was a weakling in comparison with Kitchell, the freebooter and beach-comber in sight of his prize.

"Son," said the Captain, making a bundle of all the papers, "take these over to my bunk and hide 'em under the donkey's breakfast. Stop a bit," he added, as Wilbur started away. "I'll go with you. We'll have to bury the old man."

Throughout all the afternoon the Captain had been drinking the whiskey from the decanter found in the cabin; now he stood up unsteadily, and, raising his glass, exclaimed:

"Sonny, here's to Kitchell, Wilbur & Co., beach-combers, un-limited. What do you say, hey?"

"I only want to be sure that we've a right to the bark," answered Wilbur.

"Right to her—ri-hight to 'er," hiccoughed the Captain. "Strike me blind, I'd like to see any one try'n take her away from Alvinza Kitchell now," and he thrust out his chin at Wilbur.

"Well, so much the better, then," said

Wilbur, pocketing the papers. The pair ascended to the deck.

The burial of Captain Sternersen was a dreadful business. Kitchell, far gone in whiskey, stood on the house issuing his orders, drinking from one of the decanters he had brought up with him. He had already rifled the dead man's pockets, and had even taken away the boots and fur-lined cap. Cloths were cut from the spanker and rolled around the body. Then Kitchell ordered the peak halyards unrove and used as lashings to tie the canvas around the corpse. The red and white flags (the distress signals) were still bound on the halyards.

"Leave 'em on. Leave 'em on," commanded Kitchell. "Use 'm as a shrou'. All ready now, stan' by to let her go."

Wilbur looked over at the schooner and noted with immense relief that Moran was not in sight. Suddenly an abrupt reaction took place in the Captain's addled brain.

"Can't bury 'um 'ithout 'is teeth," he gabbled solemnly. He laid back the canvas and replaced the set. "Ole man'd ha'nt me 'f I kep' 's teeth. Strike! look a' that, I put 'em in upside down. Nev' min', upsi' down, downsi' up, whaz odds, all same with ole Bill, hey, ole Bill, all same with you, hey?" Suddenly he began to howl with laughter. "T' think a bein' buried with yo'r teeth upsi' down. Oh, mee, but that's a good grind. Stan' by to heave ole Uncle Bill over—ready, heave, an' away she goes." He ran to the side, waving his hat and looking over. "Goo'-by, ole Bill, by-by. There you go, an' the signal o' distress roun' you, H. B. 'I'm in need of assistance.' Lord, here comes the sharks—look! look! look at um fight! look at um takin' ole Bill! I'm in need of assistance. I sh'd say you were, ole Bill."

Wilbur looked once over the side in the churning, lashing water, then drew back, sick to vomiting. But in less than thirty seconds the water was quiet. Not a shark was in sight.

"Get over t' the *Bertha* with those papers, son," ordered Kitchell; "I'll bide here and dig up sh' mor loot. I'll gut this ole pill-box from stern to stem-post 'fore I'll leave. I won't leave a copper rivet in 'er, notta co'er rivet, dyhear?" he shouted, his face purple with unnecessary rage.

Wilbur returned to the schooner with the two Chinamen, leaving Kitchell alone on the bark. He found the girl sitting by the rudderhead almost as he had left her, looking about her with vague, unseeing eyes.

"Your name is Moran, isn't it?" he asked. "Moran Sternersen."

"Yes," she said, after a pause, then looked curiously at a bit of tarred rope on the deck. Nothing more could be got out of her. Wilbur talked to her at length, and tried to make her understand the situation, but it was evident she did not follow. However, at each mention of her name she would answer:

"Yes, yes, I'm Moran."

Wilbur turned away from her, biting his nether lip in perplexity.

"Now, what am I going to do?" he muttered. "What a situation! If I tell the Captain, it's all up with the girl. If he didn't kill her, he'd do worse—might do both. If I don't tell him, there goes her birthright, $60,000, and she alone in the world. It's begun to go already," he added, listening to the sounds that came from the bark. Kitchell was raging to and fro in the cabin in a frenzy of drink, axe in hand, smashing glassware, hacking into the woodwork, singing the while at the top of his voice:

"As through the drop I go, drop I go,
As through the drop I go, drop I go,
As through the drop I go,
Down to hell that yawns below,
Twenty stiffs all in a row,
Damn your eyes."

"That's the kind of man I have to deal

with," muttered Wilbur. "It's encouraging, and there's no one to talk to. Not much help in a Chinaman and a crazy girl in a man's oilskins. It's about the biggest situation you ever faced, Ross Wilbur, and you're all alone. What the devil are you going to do?"

He acknowledged with considerable humiliation that he could not get the better of Kitchell, either physically or mentally. Kitchell was a more powerful man than he, and cleverer. The Captain was in his element now, and he was the commander. On shore it would have been vastly different. The city-bred fellow, with a policeman always in call, would have known how to act.

"I simply can't stand by and see that hog plundering everything she's got. What's to be done?"

And suddenly, while the words were yet in his mouth, the sun was wiped from the sky like writing from a slate, the horizon blackened, vanished, a long white line of froth whipped across the sea and came on hissing. A hollow note boomed out, boomed, swelled, and grew rapidly to a roar.

An icy chill stabbed the air. Then the squall swooped and struck, and the sky shut down over the troubled ocean like a pot-lid over a boiling pot. The schooner's fore and main sheets, that had not been made fast, unrove at the first gust and began to slat wildly in the wind. The Chinamen cowered to the decks, grasping at cleats, stays, and masts. They were helpless — paralyzed with fear. Charlie clung to a stay, one arm over his head, as though dodging a blow. Wilbur gripped the rail with his hands where he stood, his teeth set, his eyes wide, waiting for the foundering of the schooner, his only thought being that the end could not be far. He had heard of the suddenness of tropical squalls, but this had come with the abruptness of a scene-shift at a play. The schooner veered broad-on to

the waves. It was the beginning of the
end—another roll to the leeward like the
last and the Pacific would come aboard.

"And you call ourselves sailor men!
Are you going to drown like rats on a
plank?" A voice that Wilbur did not
know went ringing through that horrid
shouting of wind and sea like the call of
a bugle. He turned to see Moran, the
girl of the *Lady Letty*, standing erect
upon the quarterdeck, holding down the
schooner's wheel. The confusion of that
dreadful moment, that had paralyzed the
crew's senses, had brought back hers.
She was herself again, savage, splendid,
dominant, superb in her wrath at their
weakness, their cowardice.

Her heavy brows were knotted over
her flaming eyes, her hat was gone, and
her thick bands of yellow hair whipped
across her face and streamed out in the
wind like streamers of the northern lights.
As she shouted, gesturing furiously to the
men, the loose skin of the oilskin coat

fell back, and showed her forearm, strong, round, and white as scud, the hand and wrist so tanned as to look almost like a glove. And all the while she shouted aloud, furious with indignation, raging against the supineness of the *Bertha's* crew.

"Stand by, men! stand by! Look alive, now! Make fast the stays'l halyards to the dory's warp! Now, then, unreeve y'r halyards! all clear there! pass the end for'd outside the rigging! outside! you fools! Make fast to the bits for'ard—let go y'r line—that'll do. Soh —soh. There, she's coming up."

The dory had been towing astern, and the seas combing over her had swamped her. Moran had been inspired to use the swamped boat as a sea-anchor, fastening her to the schooner's bow instead of to the stern. The *Bertha's* bow, answering to the drag, veered around. The *Bertha* stood head to the seas, riding out the squall. It was a masterpiece of seamanship, conceived and executed in the very thick of peril, and it saved the schooner.

But there was little time to think of themselves. On board the bark the sails were still set. The squall struck the *Lady Letty* squarely aback. She heeled over upon the instant; then as the top hamper carried away with a crash, eased back a moment upon an even keel. But her cargo had shifted. The bark was doomed. Through the flying spray and scud and rain Wilbur had a momentary glimpse of Kitchell, hacking at the lanyards with his axe. Then the *Lady Letty* capsized, going over till her masts were flat with the water, and in another second rolled bottom up. For a moment her keel and red iron bottom were visible through the mist of driving spoon-drift. Suddenly they sank from sight. She was gone.

And then, like the rolling up of a scroll, the squall passed, the sun returned, the sky burned back to blue, the ruggedness was smoothed from the ocean, and the warmth of the tropics closed around the *Bertha Millner*, once more rolling easily on the swell of the ocean.

Of the *Lady Letty* and the drunken beach-combing Captain not a trace remained. Kitchell had gone down with his prize. The *Bertha Millner's* Chinese crew huddled forward, talking wildly, pointing and looking in a bewildered fashion over the sides.

Wilbur and Moran were left alone on the open Pacific.

V

A Girl Captain

WHEN Wilbur came on deck the morning after the sinking of the bark he was surprised to find the schooner under way again. Wilbur and Charlie had berthed forward during that night—Charlie with the hands, Wilbur in the Captain's hammock. The reason for this change of quarters had been found in a peremptory order from Moran during the dog-watch the preceding evening.

She had looked squarely at Wilbur from under her scowl, and had said briefly and in a fine contralto voice, that he had for the first time noted: "I berth aft, in the cabin; you and the Chinaman forward. Understand?"

Moran had only forestalled Wilbur's intention; while after her almost miraculous piece of seamanship in the rescue of the schooner, Charlie and the Chinese crew accorded her a respect that was almost superstitious.

Wilbur met her again at breakfast. She was still wearing men's clothing— part of Kitchell's outfit—and was booted to the knee; but now she wore no hat, and her enormous mane of rye-colored hair was braided into long strands near to the thickness of a man's arm. The redness of her face gave a startling effect to her pale blue eyes and sandy, heavy eyebrows, that easily lowered to a frown. She ate with her knife, and after pushing away her plate Wilbur observed that she drank half a tumbler of whiskey and water.

The conversation between the two was tame enough. There was no common ground upon which they could meet. To her father's death—no doubt an old matter even before her rescue—she made no allusion. Her attitude toward Wilbur was one of defiance and suspicion. Only once did she relax:

"How did you come to be aboard here with these rat-eaters—you're no sailor?" she said abruptly.

"Huh!" laughed Wilbur, mirthlessly; "huh! I was shanghaied."

Moran smote the table with a red fist, and shouted with sonorous, bell-toned laughter:

"Shanghaied?—you? Now, that is really good. And what are you going to do now?"

"What are you going to do?"

"Signal the first home-bound vessel and be taken into Frisco. I've my insurance to collect (Wilbur had given her the *Letty's* papers) and the disaster to report."

"Well, I'm not keen on shark-hunting myself," said Wilbur. But Moran showed no interest in his plans.

However, they soon found that they were not to be permitted to signal. At

noon the same day the schooner sighted
a steamship's smoke on the horizon, and
began to raise her rapidly. Moran immediately bound on the ensign, union
down, and broke it out at the peak.

Charlie, who was at the wheel, spoke
a sentence in Chinese, and one of the
hands drew his knife across the halyards
and brought the distress signal to the
deck. Moran turned upon Charlie with
an oath, her brows knotted.

"No! No!" sang Charlie, closing his
eyes and wagging his head; "No! Too
muchee los' time; no can stop. You
come down-side cabin; you an' one-piece
boss number two (this was Wilbur) have
um chin-chin."

The odd conclave assembled about
Kitchell's table—the clubman, the half-
masculine girl in men's clothes, and the
Chinaman. The conference was an angry one, Wilbur and Moran insisting that
they be put aboard the steamship, Charlie
refusing with calm obstinacy.

A Girl Captain

"I have um chin-chin with China boys las' nigh'. China boy heap flaid, no can stop um steamship. Heap flaid too much talkee-talkee. No stop; go fish now; go fish chop-chop. Los' heap time; go fish. I no savvy sail um boat, China boy no savvy sail um boat. I tink um you savvy (and he pointed to Moran). I tink um you savvy plenty heap much disa bay. Boss number two, no savvy sail um boat, but him savvy plenty many all same."

"And we're to stop on board your dough-dish and navigate her for you?" shouted Moran, her face blazing.

Charlie nodded blandly: "I tink um yass."

"And when we get back to port," exclaimed Wilbur, "you think, perhaps, I—we won't make it interesting for you?"

Charlie smiled.

"I tink um Six Company heap rich."

"Well, get along," ordered Moran, as

though the schooner was her property, "and we'll talk it over."

"China boy lika you heap pretty big," said Charlie to Moran, as he went out. "You savvy sail um boat all light; wanta you fo' captain. But," he added, suddenly dropping his bland passivity as though it were a mask, and for an instant allowing the wicked malevolent Cantonese to come to the surface, "China boy no likee funnee business, savvy?" Then with the smile of a Talleyrand he disappeared.

Moran and Wilbur were helpless for the present. They were but two against seven Chinamen. They must stay on board, if the coolies wished it; and if they were to stay it was a matter of their own personal safety that the *Bertha Millner* should be properly navigated.

"I'll captain her," concluded Moran, sullenly, at the end of their talk. "You must act as mate, Mr. Wilbur. And **don't get** any mistaken idea into your head that, because I'm a young girl and alone, you are going to run things your way. I don't like funny business any better than Charlie."

"Look here," said Wilbur, complaining, "don't think I'm altogether a villain. I think you're a ripping fine girl. You're different from any kind of girl I ever met, of course, but you, by jingo, you're —you're splendid. There in the squall last evening, when you stood at the wheel, with your hair——"

"Oh, drop that!" said the girl, contemptuously, and went up on deck. Wilbur followed, scratching an ear.

Charlie was called aft and their decision announced. Moran would navigate the *Bertha Millner*, Wilbur and she taking the watches. Charlie promised that he would answer for the obedience of the men.

Their first concern now was to shape their course for Magdalena Bay. Moran and Wilbur looked over Kitchell's charts and log-book, but the girl flung them aside disdainfully.

" He's been sailing by the dead reckoning, and his navigation is drivel. Why, a cabin-boy would know better; and, to end with, the chronometer is run down. I'll have to get Green'ich time by taking the altitude of a star to-night, and figure out our longitude. Did you bring off our sextant?"

Wilbur shook his head. " Only the papers," he said.

" There's only an old ebony quadrant here," said Moran, " but it will have to do."

That night, lying flat on her back on the deck with the quadrant to her eye, she "got a star and brought it down to the horizon," and sat up under the reeking lamp in the cabin nearly the whole night ciphering and ciphering till she had filled up the four sides of the log-slate with her calculations. However, by daylight she had obtained the correct Greenwich time and worked the schooner's longitude.

Two days passed, then a third. Moran set the schooner's course. She kept almost entirely to herself, and when not at the wheel or taking the sun or writing up the log, gloomed over the after-rail into the schooner's wake. Wilbur knew not what to think of her. Never in his life had he met with any girl like this. So accustomed had she been to the rough, give-and-take, direct associations of a seafaring life that she misinterpreted wellmeant politeness—the only respect he knew how to pay her—to mean insidious advances. She was suspicious of him—distrusted him utterly, and openly ridiculed his abortive seamanship. Pretty she was not, but she soon began to have a certain amount of attraction for Wilbur. He liked her splendid ropes of hair, her heavy contralto voice, her fine animal strength of bone and muscle (admittedly greater than his own); he admired her

indomitable courage and self-reliance,
while her positive genius in the matters
of seamanship and navigation filled him
with speechless wonder. The girls he had
been used to were clever only in their
knowledge of the amenities of an afternoon call or the formalities of a paper german. A girl of two-and-twenty who could
calculate longitude from the altitude of
a star was outside his experience. The
more he saw of her the more he knew
himself to have been right in his first
estimate. She drank whiskey after her
meals, and when angry, which was often,
swore like a buccaneer. As yet she was
almost, as one might say, without sex—
savage, unconquered, untamed, glorying
in her own independence, her sullen isolation. Her neck was thick, strong, and
very white, her hands roughened and calloused. In her men's clothes she looked
tall, vigorous, and unrestrained, and on
more than one occasion, as Wilbur passed
close to her, he was made aware that her

hair, her neck, her entire personality exhaled a fine, sweet, natural redolence that savored of the ocean and great winds.

One day, as he saw her handling a huge water-barrel by the chines only, with a strength he knew to be greater than his own, her brows contracted with the effort, her hair curling about her thick neck, her large, round arms bare to the elbow, a sudden thrill of enthusiasm smote through him, and between his teeth he exclaimed to himself:

"By Jove, you're a woman!"

The *Bertha Millner* continued to the southward, gliding quietly over the oil-smoothness of the ocean under airs so light as hardly to ruffle the surface. Sometimes at high noon the shimmer of the ocean floor blended into the shimmer of the sky at the horizon, and then it was no longer water and blue heavens; the little craft seemed to be poised in a vast crystalline sphere, where there was neither height nor depth—poised motionless in warm, coruscating, opalescent space, alone with the sun.

At length one morning the schooner, which for the preceding twenty-four hours had been heading eastward, raised the land, and by the middle of the afternoon had come up to within a mile of a low, sandy shore, quivering with heat, and had tied up to the kelp in Magdalena Bay.

Charlie now took over entire charge of operations. For two days previous the Chinese hands had been getting out the deck-tubs, tackles, gaffs, spades, and the other shark-fishing gear that had been stowed forward. The sails were lowered and gasketted, the decks cleared of all impedimenta, hogsheads and huge vats stood ready in the waist, and the lazy indolence of the previous week was replaced by an extraordinary activity.

The day after their arrival in the bay was occupied by all hands in catching bait. This bait was a kind of rock-fish, of a beautiful red gold color, and about the size of an ordinary cod. They bit readily enough, but out of every ten hooked three were taken off the lines by the sharks before they could be brought aboard. Another difficulty lay in the fact that, either because of the excessive heat in the air or the percentage of alkali in the water, they spoiled almost immediately if left in the air.

Turtle were everywhere—floating gray-green discs just under the surface. Sea-birds in clouds clamored all day long about the shore and sand-spits. At long intervals flying-fish skittered over the water like skipping-stones. Shoals of porpoises came in from outside, leaping clumsily along the edges of the kelp. Bewildered land-birds perched on the schooner's rigging, and in the early mornings the whistling of quail could be heard on shore near where a little fresh-water stream ran down to meet the ocean.

It was Wilbur who caught the first shark on the second morning of the *Ber-*

tha's advent in Magdalena Bay. A store
of bait had been accumulated, split and
halved into chunks for the shark-hooks,
and Wilbur, baiting one of the huge lines
that had been brought up on deck the
evening before, flung it overboard, and
watched the glimmer of the white fish-
meat turning to a silvery green as it sank
down among the kelp. Almost instantly
a long moving shadow, just darker than
the blue-green mass of the water, identi-
fied itself at a little distance.

Enormous flukes proceeded from either
side, an erect dorsal fin, like an enormous
cock's crest, rose from the back, while immediately over the head swam the two
pilot-fish, following so closely the movement of the shark as to give the impression
of actually adhering to his body. Twice
and three times the great man-eater, twelve
feet from snout to tail-tip, circled slowly
about the bait, the flukes moving fan-like
through the water. Once he came up,
touched the bait with his nose, and backed

easily away. He disappeared, returned, and poised himself motionless in the schooner's shadow, feeling the water with his flukes.

Moran was looking over Wilbur's shoulder. "He's as good as caught," she muttered; "once let them get sight of meat, and—— Steady now!" The shark moved forward. Suddenly, with a long, easy roll, he turned completely upon his back. His white belly flashed like silver in the water—the bait disappeared.

"You've got him!" shouted Moran.

The rope slid through Wilbur's palms, burning the skin as the huge sea-wolf sounded. Moran laid hold. The heavy, sullen wrenching from below twitched and swayed their bodies and threw them against each other. Her bare, cool arm was pressed close over his knuckles.

"Heave!" she cried, laughing with the excitement of the moment. "Heave all!" —she began the chant of sailors hauling at the ropes. Together, and bracing their feet against the schooner's rail, they fought out the fight with the great fish. In a swirl of lather the head and shoulders came above the surface, the flukes churning the water till it boiled like the wake of a screw steamship. But as soon as these great fins were clear of the surface the shark fell quiet and helpless.

Charlie came up with the cutting-in spade, and as the fish hung still over the side, cut him open from neck to belly with a single movement. Another Chinaman stood by with a long-handled gaff, hooked out the purple-black liver, brought it over the side, and dropped it into one of the deck-tubs. The shark thrashed and writhed, his flukes quivering and his gills distended. Wilbur could not restrain an exclamation.

" Brutal business!" he muttered.

"Hoh!" exclaimed Moran, scornfully, " cutting-in is too good for him. Sailor-folk are no friends of such carrion as that."

Other lines were baited and dropped

A Girl Captain

overboard, and the hands settled themselves to the real business of the expedition. There was no skill in the matter. The sharks bit ravenously, and soon swarmed about the schooner in hundreds. Hardly a half minute passed that one of the four Chinamen that were fishing did not signal a catch, and Charlie and Jim were kept busy with spade and gaff. By noon the deck-tubs were full. The lines were hauled in, and the hands set the tubs in the sun to try out the oil. Under the tropical heat the shark livers almost visibly melted away, and by 4 o'clock in the afternoon the tubs were full of a thick, yellow oil, the reek of which instantly recalled to Wilbur's mind the rancid smell of the schooner on the day when he had first come aboard of her. The deck-tubs were emptied into the hogsheads and vats that stood in the waist of the *Bertha*, the tubs scoured, and the lines and bent shark-hooks overhauled. Charlie disappeared in the galley, supper was cooked, and **eaten** upon deck under the conflagration of the sunset; the lights were set, the Chinamen foregathered in the fo'c'stle head, smoking opium, and by eight o'clock the routine of the day was at an end.

So the time passed. In a short time Wilbur could not have said whether the day was Wednesday or Sunday. He soon tired of the unsportsmanlike work of killing the sluggish brutes, and turned shoreward to relieve the monotony of the succeeding days. He and Moran were left a good deal to their own devices. Charlie was the master of the men now. "Mate," said Moran to Wilbur one day, after a dinner of turtle steaks and fish, eaten in the open air on the quarter-deck; "mate, this is slow work, and the schooner smells terribly foul. We'll have the dory out and go ashore. We can tumble a cask into her and get some water. The butt's three-quarters empty. Let's see how it feels to be in Mexico."

"Mexico?" said Wilbur. "That's so

—Lower California is Mexico. I'd forgotten that!"

They went ashore and spent the afternoon in filling the water-cask from the
fresh-water stream and in gathering abalones, which Moran declared were delicious eating, from the rocks left bare by
the tide. But nothing could have ex-
ceeded the loneliness of that shore and
backland, palpitating under the flogging
of a tropical sun. Low hills of sand,
covered with brush, stretched back from
the shore. On the eastern horizon,
leagues distant, blue masses of moun-
tains, striated with mirages, swam in the
scorching air.

The sand was like fire to the touch.
Far out in the bay the schooner hung
motionless under bare sticks, resting ap-
parently upon her inverted shadow only.
And that was all—the flat, heat-ridden
land, the sheen of the open Pacific, and
the lonely schooner.

"Quiet enough," said Wilbur, in a low

voice, wondering if there was such a place as San Francisco, with its paved streets and cable cars, and if people who had been his friends there had ever had any real existence.

"Do you like it?" asked Moran quickly, facing him, her thumbs in her belt.

"It's good fun,—how about you?"

"It's no different than the only life I've known. I suppose you think it's a queer kind of life for a girl. I've lived by doing things, not by thinking things, or reading about what other people have done or thought; and I guess it's what you do that counts, rather than what you think or read about. Where's that pinch-bar? We'll get a couple more abalones for supper, and then put off."

That was the only talk of moment they had during the afternoon. All the rest of their conversation had been of those things that immediately occupied their attention.

They regained the schooner toward five

o'clock, to find the Chinamen perplexed and mystified. No explanation was forthcoming, and Charlie gave them supper in preoccupied silence. As they were eating the abalones, which Moran had fried in batter, Charlie said:

"Shark all gone! No more catch um —him all gone."

"Gone—why?"

"No savvy," said Charlie. "No likee, no likee. China boy tink um heap funny, too much heap funny."

It was true. During all the next day not a shark was in sight, and though the crew fished assiduously till dark, they were rewarded by not so much as a bite. No one could offer any explanation.

"'Tis strange," said Moran. "Never heard of shark leaving this feed before. And you can see with half an eye that the hands don't like the looks of it. Superstitious beggars! they need to be clumped in the head."

That same night Wilbur woke in his

hammock on the fo'c'stle head about half-past two. The moon was down, the sky one powder of stars. There was not a breath of wind. It was so still that he could hear some large fish playing and breaking off toward the shore. Then, without the least warning, he felt the schooner begin to lift under him. He rolled out of his hammock and stood on the deck. There could be no doubt of it—the whole forepart was rising beneath him. He could see the bowsprit moving upward from star to star. Still the schooner lifted; objects on deck began to slide aft; the oil in the deck-tubs washed over; then, as there came a wild scrambling of the Chinese crew up the fo'c'stle hatch, she settled again gradually at first, then, with an abrupt lurch that almost threw him from his feet, regained her level. Moran met him in the waist. Charlie came running aft.

"What was that? Are we grounding? Has she struck?"

"No, no; we're still fast to the kelp. Was it a tidal wave?"

"Nonsense. It wouldn't have handled us that way."

"Well, what was it? Listen! For God's sake keep quiet there forward!"

Wilbur looked over the side into the water. The ripples were still chasing themselves away from the schooner. There was nothing else. The stillness shut down again. There was not a sound.

VI

A Sea Mystery

In spite of his best efforts at self-control, Wilbur felt a slow, cold clutch at his heart. That sickening, uncanny lifting of the schooner out of the glassy water, at a time when there was not enough wind to so much as wrinkle the surface, sent a creep of something very like horror through all his flesh.

Again he peered over the side, down into the kelp-thickened sea. Nothing— not a breath of air was stirring. The gray light that flooded down from the stars showed not a break upon the surface of Magdalena Bay. On shore, nothing moved.

"Quiet there, forward," called Moran to the shrill-voiced coolies.

The succeeding stillness was profound.

A Sea Mystery

All on board listened intently. The water dripped like the ticking of a clock from the *Bertha Millner's* stern, which with the rising of the bow had sunk almost to the rail. There was no other sound.

"Strange," muttered Moran, her brows contracting.

Charlie broke the silence with a wail: "No likee, no likee!" he cried at top voice.

The man had gone suddenly green; Wilbur could see the shine of his eyes distended like those of a harassed cat. As he, Moran, and Wilbur stood in the schooner's waist, staring at each other, the smell of punk came to their nostrils. Forward, the coolies were already burning joss-sticks on the fo'castle head, kowtowing their foreheads to the deck.

Moran went forward and kicked them to their feet and hurled their joss-sticks into the sea.

"Feng shui! Feng shui!" they exclaimed with bated breaths. "The Feng shui no likee we."

Low in the east the horizon began to blacken against the sky. It was early morning. A watch was set, the Chinamen sent below, and until daybreak, when Charlie began to make a clattering of tins in the galley as he set about preparing breakfast, Wilbur paced the rounds of the schooner, looking, listening, and waiting again for that slow, horrifying lift. But the rest of the night was without incident.

After breakfast, the strangely assorted trio—Charlie, Moran, and Wilbur—held another conference in the cabin. It was decided to move the schooner to the other side of the bay.

"Feng shui in disa place, no likee we," announced Charlie.

"Feng shui, who are they?"

Charlie promptly became incoherent on this subject, and Moran and Wilbur could only guess that the Feng shui were the

tutelary deities that presided over that
portion of Magdalena Bay. At any rate,
there were evidently no more shark to be
caught in that fishing-ground; so sail was
made, and by noon the *Bertha Millner*
tied up to the kelp on the opposite side
of the inlet, about half a mile from the
shore.

The shark were plentiful here, and the
fishing went forward again as before.
Certain of these shark were hauled
aboard, stunned by a blow on the nose,
and their fins cut off. The Chinamen
packed these fins away in separate kegs.
Eventually they would be sent to China.

Two or three days passed. The hands
kept steadily at their work. Nothing
more occurred to disturb the monotony of
the scorching days and soundless nights;
the schooner sat as easily on the unbroken water as though built to the
bottom. Soon the night watch was dis-
continued. During these days the three
officers lived high. Turtle were plenti-

ful, and what with their steaks and soups, the fried abalones, the sea-fish, the really delicious shark-fins, and the quail that Charlie and Wilbur trapped along the shore, the trio had nothing to wish for in the way of table luxuries.

The shore was absolutely deserted, as well as the back country—an unbroken wilderness of sand and sage. Half a dozen times, Wilbur, wearying of his inaction aboard the schooner, made the entire circuit of the bay from point to point. Standing on one of the latter projections and looking out to the west, the Pacific appeared as empty of life as the land. Never a keel cut those waters, never a sail broke the edge of the horizon, never a feather of smoke spotted the sky where it whitened to meet the sea. Everything was empty—vast unspeakably desolate—palpitating with heat.

Another week passed. Charlie began to complain that the shark were growing scarce again.

A Sea Mystery

"I think bime-by him go way, once a mo'."

That same night, Wilbur, lying in his hammock, was awakened by a touch on his arm. He woke to see Moran beside him on the deck.

"Did you hear anything?" she said in a low voice, looking at him under her scowl.

"No! no!" he exclaimed, getting up, reaching for his wicker sandals. "Did you?"

"I thought so—something. Did you feel anything?"

"I've been asleep, I haven't noticed anything. Is it beginning again?"

"The schooner lifted again, just now, very gently. I happened to be awake or I wouldn't have noticed it." They were talking in low voices, as is the custom of people speaking in the dark.

"There, what's that?" exclaimed Wilbur under his breath. A gentle vibration, barely perceptible, thrilled through the schooner. Under his hand, that was clasped upon the rail, Wilbur could feel a faint trembling in her frame. It stopped, began again, and died slowly away.

"Well, what the devil *is* it?" he muttered impatiently, trying to master the returning creep of dread.

Moran shook her head, biting her lip.

"It's beyond *me*," she said, frowning. "Can you see anything?" The sky, sea, and land were unbroken reaches of solitude. There was no breath of wind.

"Listen," said Moran. Far off to landward came the faint, sleepy clucking of a quail, and the stridulating of unnumbered crickets; a long ripple licked the slope of the beach and slid back into the ocean. Wilbur shook his head.

"Don't hear anything," he whispered. "Sh—there—she's trembling again."

Once more a prolonged but faint quivering ran through the *Bertha Millner* from stem to stern, and from keel to masthead. There was a barely audible creaking of joints and panels. The oil in the deck-tubs trembled. The vibration was so fine and rapid that it tickled the soles of Wilbur's feet as he stood on the deck.

"I'd give two fingers to know what it all means," murmured Moran in a low voice. "I've been to sea for——" Then suddenly she cried aloud: "Steady all, she's lifting again!"

The schooner heaved slowly under them, this time by the stern. Up she went, up and up, while Wilbur gripped at a stay to keep his place, and tried to choke down his heart, that seemed to beat against his palate.

"God!" ejaculated Moran, her eyes blazing. "This thing is——" The *Bertha* came suddenly down to an easy keel, rocking in that glassy sea as if in a tide rip. The deck was awash with oil. Far out in the bay the ripples widening from the schooner blurred the reflections of the stars. The Chinamen swarmed up the

hatchway, voluble and shrill. Again the
Bertha Millner lifted and sank, the tubs
sliding on the deck, the masts quivering
like reeds, the timbers groaning aloud
with the strain. In the stern something
cracked and smashed. Then the trouble
died away, the ripples faded into the
ocean, and the schooner settled to her
keel, quite motionless.

"Look," said Moran, her face toward
the *Bertha's* stern. "The rudder is out
of the gudgeons." It was true—the
Bertha Millner's helm was unshipped.

There was no more sleep for any one
on board that night. Wilbur tramped
the quarter-deck, sick with a feeling he
dared not put a name to. Moran sat by
the wrecked rudder-head, a useless pistol
in her hand, swearing under her breath
from time to time. Charlie appeared on
the quarter-deck at intervals, looked at
Wilbur and Moran with wide-open eyes,
and then took himself away. On the
forward deck the coolies pasted strips of

red paper inscribed with mottoes upon the mast, and filled the air with the reek of their joss-sticks.

"If one could only *see* what it was," growled Moran between her clenched teeth. "But this—this damned heaving and trembling, it—it's queer."

"That's it, that's it," said Wilbur quickly, facing her. "What are we going to do, Moran?"

"*Stick it out!*" she exclaimed, striking her knee with her fist. "We can't leave the schooner — I *won't* leave her. I'll stay by this dough-dish as long as two planks in her hold together. Were you thinking of cutting away?" She fixed him with her frown.

Wilbur looked at her, sitting erect by the disabled rudder, her head bare, her braids of yellow hair hanging over her breast, sitting there in man's clothes and man's boots, the pistol at her side. He shook his head.

"I'm not leaving the *Bertha* till you do," he answered; adding: "I'll stand by you, mate, until we——"

"Feel that?" said Moran, holding up a hand.

A fine, quivering tremble was thrilling through every beam of the schooner, vibrating each rope like a harp-string. It passed away; but before either Wilbur or Moran could comment upon it recommenced, this time much more perceptibly. Charlie dashed aft, his queue flying.

"W'at makum heap shake?" he shouted; "w'at for him shake? No savvy, no likee, pretty much heap flaid; aie-yah, aie-yah!"

Slowly the schooner heaved up as though upon the crest of some huge wave, slowly it settled, and again gradually lifted, till Wilbur had to catch at the rail to steady his footing. The quivering sensation increased so that their very teeth chattered with it. Below in the

128

cabin they could hear small objects falling from the shelves and table. Then with a sudden drop the *Bertha* fell back to her keel again, the spilled oil spouting from her scuppers, the masts rocking, the water churning and splashing from her sides.

And that was all. There was no sound—nothing was in sight. There was only the frightened trembling of the little schooner and that long, slow heave and lift.

Morning came, and breakfast was had in silence and grim perplexity. It was too late to think of getting away, now that the rudder was disabled. The *Bertha Millner* must bide where she was.

"And a little more of this dancing," exclaimed Moran, "and we'll have the planks springing off the stern-post."

Charlie nodded solemnly. He said nothing — his gravity had returned. Now in the glare of the tropical day, with the *Bertha Millner* sitting the sea as placidly as a brooding gull, he was Talleyrand again.

"I tinkum yas," he said vaguely.

"Well, *I* think we had better try and fix the rudder and put back to Frisco," said Moran. "You're making no money this way. There are no shark to be caught. *Something's* wrong. They're gone away somewhere. The crew are eating their heads off and not earning enough money to pay for their keep. What do you think?"

"I tinkum yas."

"Then we'll go home. Is that it?"

"I tinkum yas—to-molla."

"To-morrow?"

"Yas."

"That's settled then," persisted Moran, surprised at his ready acquiescence; "we start home to-morrow?" Charlie nodded.

"To-molla," he said.

The rudder was not so badly damaged as they had at first supposed; the break was easily mended, but it was found necessary for one of the men to go over the side.

"Get over the side here, Jim," commanded Moran. "Charlie, tell him what's wanted; we can't work the pintle in from the deck."

But Charlie shook his head.

"Him no likee go; him plenty much flaid."

Moran ripped out an oath.

"What do I care if he's afraid! I want him to shove the pintle into the lower gudgeon. My God," she exclaimed, with immense contempt, "what carrion! I'd sooner work a boat with she-monkeys. Mr. Wilbur, I shall have to ask you to go over. I thought I was captain here, but it all depends on whether these rats are afraid or not."

"Plenty many shark," expostulated Charlie. "Him flaid shark come back, catchum chop-chop."

"Stand by here with a couple of cutting-in spades," cried Moran, "and fend off if you see any shark; now, then, are you ready, mate?"

Wilbur took his determination in both hands, threw off his coat and sandals, and went over the stern rail.

"Put your ear to the water," called Moran from above; "sometimes you can hear their flukes."

It took but a minute to adjust the pintle, and Wilbur regained the deck again, dripping and a little pale. He knew not what horrid form of death might have been lurking for him down below there underneath the kelp. As he started forward for dry clothes he was surprised to observe that Moran was smiling at him, holding out her hand.

"That was well done," she said, "and thank you. I've seen older sailor-men than you who wouldn't have taken the risk." Never before had she appeared more splendid in his eyes than at this moment. After changing his clothes in the fo'castle, he sat for a long time,

his chin in his hands, very thoughtful.
Then at length, as though voicing the
conclusion of his reflections, said aloud,
as he rose to his feet:

"But, of course, *that* is out of the
question."

He remembered that they were going
home on the next day. Within a fortnight he would be in San Francisco
again—a tax-payer, a police-protected
citizen once more. It had been good fun,
after all, this three weeks' life on the
Bertha Millner, a strange episode cut out
from the normal circle of his conven-
tional life. He ran over the incidents of
the cruise—Kitchell, the turtle hunt, the
finding of the derelict, the dead captain,
the squall, and the awful sight of the
sinking bark, Moran at the wheel, the
grewsome business of the shark-fishing,
and last of all that inexplicable lifting
and quivering of the schooner. He told
himself that now he would probably never
know the explanation of that mystery.

Moran of the Lady Letty

The day passed in preparations to put
to sea again. The deck-tubs and hogsheads were stowed below and the tackle
cleared away. By evening all was ready;
they would be under-way by daybreak
the next morning. There was a possi-
bility of their being forced to tow the
schooner out by means of the dory, so
light were the airs inside. Once beyond
the heads, however, they were sure of a
breeze.

About ten o'clock that night, the same
uncanny trembling ran through the
schooner again, and about half an hour
later she lifted gently once or twice.
But after that she was undisturbed.

Later on in the night—or rather early
in the morning—Wilbur woke suddenly
in his hammock without knowing why,
and got up and stood listening. The
Bertha Millner was absolutely quiet.
The night was hot and still; the new
moon, canted over like a sinking galleon,
was low over the horizon. Wilbur lis-

tened intently, for now at last he heard something.

Between the schooner and the shore a gentle sound of splashing came to his ears, and an occasional crack as of oars in their locks. Was it possible that a boat was there between the schooner and the land? What boat, and manned by whom?

The creaking of oarlocks and the dip of paddles was unmistakable.

Suddenly Wilbur raised his voice in a great shout:

" Boat ahoy !"

There was no answer; the noise of oars grew fainter. Moran came running out of her cabin, swinging into her coat as she ran.

" What is it—what is it?"

" A boat, I think, right off the schooner here. Hark—there—did you hear the oars?"

" You're right; call the hands, get the dory over, we'll follow that boat right up. Hello, forward there, Charlie, all hands, tumble out!"

Then Wilbur and Moran caught themselves looking into each other's eyes. At once something—perhaps the latent silence of the schooner—told them there was to be no answer. The two ran forward; Moran swung herself into the fo'-castle hatch, and without using the ladder dropped to the deck below. In an instant her voice came up to the hatch:

"The bunks are empty—they're gone—abandoned us." She came up the ladder again.

"Look," said Wilbur, as she regained the deck. "The dory's gone; they've taken it. It was our only boat; *we* can't get ashore."

"Cowardly, superstitious rats, I should have expected this. They would be chopped in bits before they would stay longer on board this boat—they and their Feng-shui."

When morning came the deserters

could be made out camped on the shore, near to the beached dory. What their intentions were could not be conjectured. Ridden with all manner of nameless Oriental superstitions, it was evident that the Chinamen preferred any hazard of fortune to remaining longer upon the schooner.

"Well, can we get along without them?" said Wilbur. "Can we two work the schooner back to port ourselves?"

"We'll try it on, anyhow, mate," said Moran; "we might get her into San Diego, anyhow."

The Chinamen had left plenty of provisions on board, and Moran cooked breakfast. Fortunately, by eight o'clock a very light westerly breeze came up. Moran and Wilbur cast off the gaskets and set the fore and main sails.

Wilbur was busy at the forward bitts preparing to cast loose from the kelp, and Moran had taken up her position at the wheel, when suddenly she exclaimed:

Moran of the Lady Letty

"Sail ho!—and in God's name what kind of a sail do you call it?"

In fact a strange-looking craft had just made her appearance at the entrance of Magdalena Bay.

VII

Beachcombers

Wilbur returned aft and joined Moran on the quarter-deck. She was already studying the stranger through the glass.

"That's a new build of boat to me," she muttered, giving Wilbur the glass. Wilbur looked long and carefully. The newcomer was of the size and much the same shape as a caravel of the fifteenth century—high as to bow and stern, and to all appearances as seaworthy as a soup-tureen. Never but in the old prints had Wilbur seen such an extraordinary boat. She carried a single mast, which listed forward; her lugsail was stretched upon dozens of bamboo yards; she drew hardly any water. Two enormous red eyes were painted upon either side of her high, blunt bow, while just abaft the

waist projected an enormous oar, or
sweep, full forty feet in length—longer,
in fact, than the vessel herself. It acted
partly as a propeller, partly as a rudder.

"They're heading for us," commented
Wilbur as Moran took the glass again.

"Right," she answered; adding upon
the moment: "Huh! more Chinamen;
the thing is alive with coolies; she's a
junk."

"Oh!" exclaimed Wilbur, recollecting
some talk of Charlie's he had overheard.
"I know."

"You know?"

"Yes; these are real beachcombers.
I've heard of them along this coast—
heard our Chinamen speak of them.
They beach that junk every night and
camp on shore. They're scavengers, as
you might say—pick up what they can
find or plunder along shore—abalones,
shark-fins, pickings of wrecks, old brass
and copper, seals, perhaps, turtle and
shell. Between whiles they fish for

shrimp, and I've heard Kitchell tell how
they make pearls by dropping bird-shot
into oysters. They are Kai-gingh to a
man, and, according to Kitchell, the
wickedest breed of cats that ever cut
teeth."

The junk bore slowly down upon the
schooner. In a few moments she had hove
to alongside. But for the enormous red
eyes upon her bow she was innocent of
paint. She was grimed and shellacked
with dirt and grease, and smelt abominably. Her crew were Chinamen; but
such Chinamen! The coolies of the *Bertha Millner* were pampered and effete in
comparison. The beachcombers, thir-
teen in number, were a smaller class of
men, their faces almost black with tan
and dirt. Though they still wore the
queue, their heads were not shaven,
and mats and mops of stiff black hair
fell over their eyes from under their
broad, basket-shaped hats.

They were barefoot. None of them

wore more than two garments—the jeans
and the blouse. They were the lowest
type of men Wilbur had ever seen. The
faces were those of a higher order of
anthropoid apes: the lower portion—
jaws, lips, and teeth—salient; the nostrils opening at almost right angles, the
eyes tiny and bright, the forehead seamed
and wrinkled — unnaturally old. Their
general expression was one of simian
cunning and a ferocity that was utterly
devoid of courage.

"Aye!" exclaimed Moran between her
teeth, "if the devil were a shepherd, here
are his sheep. You don't come aboard
this schooner, my friends! I want to
live as long as I can, and die when I
can't help it. Boat ahoy!" she called.

An answer in Cantonese sing-song
came back from the junk, and the
speaker gestured toward the outside
ocean.

Then a long parleying began. For
upward of half an hour Moran and Wil-

bur listened to a proposition in broken
pigeon-English made by the beachcombers again and again and yet again, and
were in no way enlightened. It was impossible to understand. Then at last
they made out that there was question of
a whale. Next it appeared the whale
was dead; and finally, after a prolonged
pantomime of gesturing and pointing,
Moran guessed that the beachcombers
wanted the use of the *Bertha Millner* to
trice up the dead leviathan while the oil
and whalebone were extracted.

"That must be it," she said to Wilbur.
"That's what they mean by pointing to
our masts and tackle. You see, they
couldn't manage with that stick of theirs,
and they say they'll give us a third of the
loot. We'll do it, mate, and I'll tell you
why. The wind has fallen, and they
can tow us out. If it's a sperm-whale
they've found, there ought to be thirty or
forty barrels of oil in him, let alone the
blubber and bone. Oil is at $50 now, and

spermaceti will always bring $100. We'll take it on, mate, but we'll keep our eyes on the rats all the time. I don't want them aboard at all. Look at their belts. Not three out of the dozen who aren't carrying those filthy little hatchets. Faugh!" she exclaimed, with a shudder of disgust. "Such vipers!"

What followed proved that Moran had guessed correctly. A rope was passed to the *Bertha Millner*, the junk put out its sweep, and to a wailing, eldritch chanting the schooner was towed out of the bay.

"I wonder what Charlie and our China boys will think of this?" said Wilbur, looking shoreward, where the deserters could be seen gathered together in a silent, observing group.

"We're well shut of them," growled Moran, her thumbs in her belt. "Only, now we'll never know what was the matter with the schooner these last few nights. Hah!" she exclaimed under her

144

breath, her scowl thickening, "sometimes
I don't wonder the beasts cut."

The dead whale was lying four miles
out of the entrance of Magdalena Bay,
and as the junk and the schooner drew
near seemed like a huge black boat floating bottom up. Over it and upon it
swarmed and clamored thousands of sea-
birds, while all around and below the
water was thick with gorging sharks. A
dreadful, strangling decay fouled all the
air.

The whale was a sperm-whale, and
fully twice the length of the *Bertha
Millner*. The work of tricing him up
occupied the beachcombers throughout
the entire day. It was out of the question to keep them off the schooner, and
Wilbur and Moran were too wise to try.
They swarmed the forward deck and rigging like a plague of unclean monkeys,
climbing with an agility and nimbleness
that made Wilbur sick to his stomach.
They were unlike any Chinamen he had

ever seen—hideous to a degree that he had imagined impossible in a human being. On two occasions a fight developed, and in an instant the little hatchets were flashing like the flash of a snake's fangs. Toward the end of the day one of them returned to the junk, screaming like a stuck pig, a bit of his chin bitten off.

Moran and Wilbur kept to the quarter-deck, always within reach of the huge cutting-in spades, but the Chinese beach-combers were too elated over their prize to pay them much attention.

And indeed the dead monster proved a veritable treasure-trove. By the end of the day he had been triced up to the foremast, and all hands straining at the windlass had raised the mighty head out of the water. The Chinamen descended upon the smooth, black body, their bare feet sliding and slipping at every step. They held on by jabbing their knives into the hide as glacier-climbers do their ice-picks. The head yielded barrel after bar-

rel of oil and a fair quantity of bone. The
blubber was taken aboard the junk, minced
up with hatchets, and run into casks.

Last of all, a Chinaman cut a hole
through the " case," and, actually descend-
ing into the inside of the head, stripped
away the spermaceti (clear as crystal), and
packed it into buckets, which were hauled
up on the junk's deck. The work occupied some two or three days. During
this time the *Bertha Millner* was keeled
over to nearly twenty degrees by the
weight of the dead monster. However,
neither Wilbur nor Moran made protest.
The Chinamen would do as they pleased;
that was said and signed. And they did
not release the schooner until the whale
had been emptied of oil and blubber,
spermaceti and bone.

At length, on the afternoon of the third
day, the captain of the junk, whose name
was Hoang, presented himself upon the
quarter - deck. He was naked to the
waist, and his bare brown torso was

gleaming with oil and sweat. His queue was coiled like a snake around his neck, his hatchet thrust into his belt.

"Well?" said Moran, coming up.

Wilbur caught his breath as the two stood there facing each other, so sharp was the contrast. The man, the Mongolian, small, weazened, leather-colored, secretive—a strange, complex creature, steeped in all the obscure mystery of the East, nervous, ill at ease; and the girl, the Anglo-Saxon, daughter of the Northmen, huge, blonde, big-boned, frank, outspoken, simple of composition, open as the day, bareheaded, her great ropes of sandy hair falling over her breast and almost to the top of her knee-boots. As he looked at the two, Wilbur asked himself where else but in California could such abrupt contrasts occur.

"All light," announced Hoang; "catchum all oil, catchum all bone, catchum all same plenty many. You help catchum, now you catchum pay. Sabe?

Beachcombers

The three principals came to a settlement with unprecedented directness. Like all Chinamen, Hoang was true to his promises, and had already set apart three and a half barrels of spermaceti, ten barrels of oil, and s me twenty pounds of bone as the schooner's share in the transaction. There was no discussion over the matter. He called their attention to the discharge of his obligations, and hurried away to summon his men aboard and get the junk under way again.

The beachcombers returned to their junk, and Wilbur and Moran set about cutting the carcass of the whale adrift. They found it would be easier to cut away the hide from around the hooks and loops of the tackle than to unfasten the tackle itself.

"The knots are jammed hard as steel," declared Moran. "Hand up that cutting-in spade; stand by with the other and cut loose at the same time as I do, so we can ease off the strain on these lines at the same time. Ready there, cut!" Moran set free the hook in the loop of black skin in a couple of strokes, but Wilbur was more clumsy; the skin resisted. He struck at it sharply with the heavy spade; the blade hit the iron hook, glanced off, and opened a large slit in the carcass below the head. A gush of entrails started from the slit, and Moran swore under breath.

"Ease away, quick there! You'll have the mast out of her next—steady! Hold your spade—what's that?"

Wilbur had nerved himself against the dreadful stench he expected would issue from the putrid monster, but he was surprised to note a pungent, sweet, and spicy odor that all at once made thick the air about him. It was an aromatic smell, stronger than that of the salt ocean, stronger even than the reek of oil and blubber from the schooner's waist—sweet as incense, penetrating as attar, delicious as a summer breeze.

"It smells pretty good, whatever it is," he answered. Moran came up to where he stood, and looked at the slit he had made in the whale's carcass. Out of it was bulging some kind of dull white matter marbled with gray. It was a hard lump of irregular shape and about as big as a hogshead.

Moran glanced over to the junk, some forty feet distant. The beach-combers were hoisting the lug-sail. Hoang was at the steering oar.

"Get that stuff aboard," she commanded quietly.

"That!" exclaimed Wilbur, pointing to the lump.

Moran's blue eyes were beginning to gleam.

"Yes, and do it before the Chinamen see you."

"But—but I don't understand."

Moran stepped to the quarter-deck, unslung the hammock in which Wilbur slept, and tossed it to him.

"Reeve it up in that; I'll pass you a line, and we'll haul it aboard. Godsend, those vermin yonder have got smells enough of their own without noticing this. Hurry, mate, I'll talk afterward."

Wilbur went over the side, and, standing as best he could upon the slippery carcass, dug out the lump and bound it up in the hammock.

"Hoh!" exclaimed Moran, with sudden exultation. "There's a lot of it. That's the biggest lump yet, I'll be bound. Is that all there is, mate?—look carefully." Her voice had dropped to a whisper.

"Yes, yes; that's all. Careful now when you haul up—Hoang has got his eye on you, and so have the rest of them. What do you call it, anyhow? Why are you so particular about it? Is it worth anything?"

"I don't know—perhaps. We'll have a look at it, anyway."

Beachcombers

Moran hauled the stuff aboard, and Wilbur followed.

"Whew!" he exclaimed with half-closed eyes. "It's like the story of Samson and the dead lion—the sweet coming forth from the strong."

The schooner seemed to swim in a bath of perfumed air; the membrane of the nostrils fairly pringled with the sensation. Moran unleashed the hammock, and going down upon one knee examined the lump attentively.

"It didn't seem possible," Wilbur heard her saying to herself; "but there can't be any mistake. It's the stuff, right enough. I've heard of such things, but this—but this——" She rose to her feet, tossing back her hair.

"Well," said Wilbur, "what do you call it?"

"The thing to do now," returned Moran, "is to get clear of here as quietly and as quickly as we can, and take this stuff with us. I can't stop to explain now, but it's big—it's big. Mate, it's big as the Bank of England."

"Those beachcombers are right on to the game, I'm afraid," said Wilbur. "Look, they're watching us. This stuff would smell across the ocean."

"Rot the beachcombers! There's a bit of wind, thank God, and we can do four knots to their one, just let us get clear once."

Moran dragged the hammock back into the cabin, and returning upon deck, helped Wilbur to cut away the last tricing tackle. The schooner righted slowly to an even keel. Meanwhile the junk had set its one lug-sail and its crew had run out the sweeps. Hoang took the steering sweep and worked the junk to a position right across the *Bertha's* bows, some fifty feet ahead.

"They're watching us, right enough," said Wilbur.

"Up your mains'l," ordered Moran. The pair set the fore and main sails with great difficulty. Moran took the wheel and Wilbur went forward to cast off the line by which the schooner had been tied up to one of the whale's flukes.

"Cut it!" cried the girl. "Don't stop to cast off."

There was a hail from the beachcombers; the port sweeps dipped and the junk bore up nearer.

"Hurry!" shouted Moran, "don't mind them. Are we clear for'rard—what's the trouble? Something's holding her." The schooner listed slowly to starboard and settled by the head.

"All clear!" cried Wilbur.

"There's something wrong!" exclaimed Moran; "she's settling for'rard." Hoang hailed the schooner a second time.

"We're still settling," called Wilbur from the bows, "what's the matter?"

"Matter that she's taking water," answered Moran wrathfully. "She's started something below, what with all that lifting and dancing and tricing up."

Wilbur ran back to the quarter-deck.

"This is a bad fix," he said to Moran. "Those chaps are coming aboard again. They're onto something, and, of course, at just this moment she begins to leak."

"They are after that ambergris," said Moran between her teeth. "Smelt it, of course,—the swine!"

"Ambergris?"

"The stuff we found in the whale. That's ambergris."

"Well?"

"Well!" shouted Moran, exasperated. "Do you know that we have found a lump that will weigh close to 250 pounds, and do you know that ambergris is selling in San Francisco at $40 an ounce? Do you know that we have picked up nearly $150,000 right out here in the ocean and are in a fair way to lose it all?"

"Can't we run for it?"

"Run for it in a boat that's taking water like a sack! Our dory's gone. Suppose we got clear of the junk, and the *Bertha* sank? Then what? If we only

156

had our crew aboard; if we were only ten to their dozen—if we were only six—by Jupiter! I'd fight them for it."

The two enormous red eyes of the junk loomed alongside and stared over into the *Bertha's* waist. Hoang and seven of the coolies swarmed aboard.

"What now?" shouted Moran, coming forward to meet them, her scowl knotting her flashing eyes together. "Is this ship yours or mine? We've done your dirty work for you. I want you clear of my deck." Wilbur stood at her side, uncertain what to do, but ready for anything she should attempt.

"I tink you catchum someting, smellum pretty big," said Hoang, his ferret glance twinkling about the schooner.

"I catchum nothing—nothing but plenty bad stink," said Moran. "No, you don't!" she exclaimed, putting herself in Hoang's way as he made for the cabin. The other beachcombers came crowding up; Wilbur even thought he saw one of them loosening his hatchet in his belt.

"This ship's mine," cried Moran, backing to the cabin door. Wilbur followed her, and the Chinamen closed down upon the pair.

"It's not much use, Moran," he muttered. "They'll rush us in a minute."

"But the ambergris is mine—is mine," she answered, never taking her eyes from the confronting coolies.

"We findum w'ale," said Hoang; "you no find w'ale; him b'long to we—eve'y-t'ing in um w'ale b'long to we, savvy?"

"No, you promised us a third of everything you found."

Even in the confusion of the moment it occurred to Wilbur that it was quite possible that at least two-thirds of the ambergris did belong to the beachcombers by right of discovery. After all, it was the beachcombers who had found the whale. He could never remember afterward whether or no he said as much to

Moran at the time. If he did, she had been deaf to it. A fury of wrath and desperation suddenly blazed in her blue eyes. Standing at her side, Wilbur could hear her teeth grinding upon each other. She was blind to all danger, animated only by a sense of injustice and imposition.

Hoang uttered a sentence in Cantonese. One of the coolies jumped forward, and Moran's fist met him in the face and brought him to his knees. Then came the rush Wilbur had foreseen. He had just time to catch a sight of Moran at grapples with Hoang when a little hatchet glinted over his head. He struck out savagely into the thick of the group—and then opened his eyes to find Moran washing the blood from his hair as he lay on the deck with his head in the hollow of her arm. Everything was quiet. The beachcombers were gone.

"Hello, what—what—what is it?" he asked, springing to his feet, his head swimming and smarting. "We had a row, didn't we? Did they hurt you? Oh, I remember; I got a cut over the head—one of their hatchet men. Did they hurt you?"

"They got the loot," she growled. "Filthy vermin! And just to make everything pleasant, the schooner's sinking."

VIII

A Run for Land

"SINKING!" exclaimed Wilbur.

Moran was already on her feet. "We'll have to beach her," she cried, "and we're six miles out. Up y'r jib, mate!" The two set the jib, flying-jib, and staysails.

The fore and main sails were already drawing, and under all the spread of her canvas the *Bertha* raced back toward the shore.

But by the time she was within the head of the bay her stern had settled to such an extent that the forefoot was clear of the water, the bowsprit pointing high into the heavens. Moran was at the wheel, her scowl thicker than ever, her eyes measuring the stretch of water that lay between the schooner and the shore.

"She'll never make it in God's world,"

11   161

she muttered as she listened to the wash of the water in the cabin under her feet. In the hold, empty barrels were afloat, knocking hollowly against each other. "We're in a bad way, mate."

"If it comes to that," returned Wilbur, surprised to see her thus easily downcast, who was usually so indomitable. "If it comes to that, we can swim for it—a couple of planks——"

"Swim?" she echoed; "I'm not thinking of that; of course we could swim."

"What then?"

"The sharks!"

Wilbur's teeth clicked sharply together. He could think of nothing to say.

As the water gained between decks the schooner's speed dwindled, and at the same time as she approached the shore the wind, shut off by the land, fell away. By this time the ocean was not four inches below the stern-rail. Two miles away was the nearest sand-spit. Wilbur broke out a distress signal on the foremast, in the hope that Charlie and the deserters might send off the dory to their assistance. But the deserters were nowhere in sight.

"What became of the junk?" he demanded suddenly of Moran. She motioned to the westward with her head. "Still laying outside."

Twenty minutes passed. Once only Moran spoke.

"When she begins to go," she said, "she'll go with a rush. Jump pretty wide, or you'll get caught in the suction."

The two had given up all hope. Moran held grimly to the wheel as a mere matter of form. Wilbur stood at her side, his clenched fists thrust into his pockets. The eyes of both were fixed on the yellow line of the distant beach. By and by Moran turned to him with an odd smile.

"We're a strange pair to die together," she said. Wilbur met her eyes an instant, but finding no reply, put his chin

in the air as though he would have told
her she might well say that.

"A strange pair to die together," Moran repeated; "but we can do that better
than we could have"—she looked away
from him—"could have *lived* together,"
she finished, and smiled again.

"And yet," said Wilbur, "these last
few weeks here on board the schooner,
we have been through a good deal—together. I don't know," he went on clumsily, "I don't know when I've been—
when I've had—I've been happier than
these last weeks. It *is* queer, isn't it?
I know, of course, what you'll say. I've
said it to myself often of late. *I* belong
to the city and to my life there, and you
—you belong to the ocean. I never
knew a girl like you—never knew a girl
could be like you. You don't know how
extraordinary it all seems to me. You
swear like a man, and you dress like a
man, and I don't suppose you've ever
been associated with other women; and

you're strong—I know you are as strong
as I am. You have no idea how different you are to the kind of girl I've
known. Imagine my kind of girl standing up before Hoang and those cutthroat
beachcombers with their knives and
hatchets. Maybe it's because you are
so unlike my kind of girl that—that
things are as they are with me. *I* don't
know. It's a queer situation. A month
or so ago I was at a tea in San Francisco, and now I'm aboard a shark-fishing
schooner sinking in Magdalena Bay; and
I'm with a girl that—that—that I—well,
I'm with *you*, and, well, *you* know how
it is—I might as well say it—I love you
more than I imagined I ever could love
a girl."

Moran's frown came back to her forehead.

"I don't like that kind of talk," she
said; "I am not used to it, and I don't
know how to take it. Believe me," she
said with a half laugh, "it's all wasted.

I never could love a man. I'm not made for men."

"No," said Wilbur, "nor for other women either."

"Nor for other women either."

Wilbur fell silent. In that instant he had a distinct vision of Moran's life and character, shunning men and shunned of women, a strange, lonely creature, solitary as the ocean whereon she lived, beautiful after her fashion; as yet without sex, proud, untamed, splendid in her savage, primal independence—a thing untouched and unsullied by civilization. She seemed to him some Bradamante, some mythical Brunhilde, some Valkyrie of the legends born out of season, lost and unfamiliar in this end-of-the-century time. Her purity was the purity of primeval glaciers. He could easily see how to such a girl the love of a man would appear only in the light of a humiliation —a degradation. And yet she *could* love, else how had *he* been able to love

her? Wilbur found himself—even at
that moment—wondering how the thing
could be done—wondering to just what
note the untouched cords would vibrate.
Just how she should be awakened one
morning to find that she—Moran, sea-
rover, virgin unconquered, without law,
without land, without sex—was, after all,
a woman.

"By God, mate!" she exclaimed of a
sudden. "The barrels are keeping us up
—the empty barrels in the hold. Hoh!
we'll make land yet."

It was true. The empty hogsheads,
destined for the storage of oil, had been
forced up by the influx of the water to
the roof of the hold, and were acting as
so many buoys—the schooner could sink
no lower. An hour later, the quarter-
deck all awash, her bow thrown high
into the air, listing horribly to starboard,
the *Bertha Millner* took ground on the
shore of Magdalena Bay at about the turn
of the tide.

Moran of the Lady Letty

Moran swung herself over the side, hip deep in the water, and, wading ashore with a line, made fast to the huge skull of a whale half buried in the sand at that point.

Wilbur followed. The schooner had grounded upon the southern horn of the bay and lay easily on a spit of sand. They could not examine the nature of the leak until low water the next morning.

"Well, here we are," said Moran, her thumbs in her belt. "What next? We may be here for two days, we *may* be here for two years. It all depends upon how bad a hole she has. Have we 'put in for repairs,' or have we been cast away, can't tell till to-morrow morning. Meanwhile, I'm hungry."

Half of the stores of the schooner were water-soaked, but upon examination Wilbur found that enough remained intact to put them beyond all fear for the present.

"There's plenty of water up the creek," he said, "and we can snare all the quail we want; and then there's the fish and abalone. Even if the stores were gone we could make out very well."

The schooner's cabin was full of water and Wilbur's hammock was gone, so the pair decided to camp on shore. In that torrid weather, to sleep in the open air was a luxury.

In great good spirits the two sat down to their first meal on land. Moran cooked a supper that, barring the absence of coffee, was delicious. The whiskey was had from aboard, and they pledged each other, standing up, in something over two stiff fingers.

"Moran," said Wilbur, "you ought to have been born a man."

"At all events, mate," she said,—"at all events, I'm not a girl."

"*No !*" exclaimed Wilbur, as he filled his pipe. "*No*, you're just Moran, Moran of the *Lady Letty*."

"And I'll stay that, too," she said decisively.

Moran of the Lady Letty

Never had an evening been more beautiful in Wilbur's eyes. There was not a breath of air. The stillness was so profound that the faint murmur of the blood behind the ear-drums became an oppression. The ocean tiptoed toward the land with tiny rustling steps. The West was one gigantic stained window, the ocean floor a solid shimmer of opalescence. Behind them, sullen purples marked the horizon, hooded with mountain crests, and after a long while the moon shrugged a gleaming shoulder into view.

Wilbur, dressed in Chinese jeans and blouse, with Chinese wicker sandals on his bare feet, sat with his back against the whale's skull, smoking quietly. For a long time there was no conversation; then at last:

"No," said Moran in a low voice. "This is the life I'm made for. In six years I've not spent three consecutive weeks on land. Now that Eilert" (she always spoke of her father by his first

name), "now that Eilert is dead, I've not
a tie, not a relative, not even a friend,
and I don't wish it."

"But the loneliness of the life, the solitude," said Wilbur, "that's what I don't
understand. Did it ever occur to you
that the best happiness is the happiness
that one shares?"

Moran clasped a knee in both hands
and looked out to sea. She never wore
a hat, and the red light of the afterglow
was turning her rye-hued hair to saffron.

"Hoh!" she exclaimed, her heavy voice
pitched even lower than usual. "Who
could understand or share any of my
pleasures, or be happy when I'm happy?
And, besides, I'm happiest when I'm
alone—I don't want any one."

"But," hesitated Wilbur, "one is not
always alone. After all, you *are* a girl,
and men, sailor-men especially, are beasts
when it's a question of a woman—an un-
protected woman."

"I'm stronger than most men," said

Moran simply. "If you, for instance, had been like some men, I should have fought you. It wouldn't have been the first time," she added, smoothing one huge braid between her palms.

Wilbur looked at her with intent curiosity—noted again, as if for the first time, the rough, blue overalls thrust into the shoes; the coarse flannel shirt open at the throat; the belt with its sheath-knife; her arms big and white and tattooed in sailor fashion; her thick, muscular neck; her red face, with its pale blue eyes and almost massive jaw; and her hair, her heavy, yellow, fragrant hair, that lay over her shoulder and breast, coiling and looping in her lap.

"No," he said, with a long breath, "I don't make it out. I knew you were out of my experience, but I begin to think now that you are out of even my imagination. You are right, you *should* keep to yourself. You should be alone—your mate isn't made yet. You are splendid

just as you are," while under his breath
he added, his teeth clenching, "and God!
but I love you."

It was growing late, the stars were
all out, the moon riding high. Moran
yawned:

"Mate, I think I'll turn in. We'll
have to be at that schooner early in the
morning, and I make no doubt she'll give
us plenty to do." Wilbur hesitated to
reply, waiting to take his cue from what
next she should say. "It's hot enough to
sleep where we are," she added, "without
going aboard the *Bertha*, though we might
have a couple of blankets off to lie on.
This sand's as hard as a plank."

Without answering, Wilbur showed her
a couple of blanket-rolls he had brought
off while he was unloading part of the
stores that afternoon. They took one
apiece and spread them on the sand by
the bleached whale's skull. Moran pulled
off her boots and stretched herself upon
her blanket with absolute unconcern, her

hands clasped under her head. Wilbur rolled up his coat for a pillow and settled himself for the night with an assumed self-possession. There was a long silence. Moran yawned again.

"I pulled the heel off my boot this morning," she said lazily, "and I've been limping all day."

"I noticed it," answered Wilbur. "Kitchell had a new pair aboard somewhere, if they're not spoiled by the water now."

"Yes?" she said indifferently; "we'll look them up in the morning."

Again there was silence.

"I wonder," she began again, staring up into the dark, "if Charlie took that frying-pan off with him when he went?"

"I don't know. He probably did."

"It was the only thing we had to cook abalones in. Make me think to look into the galley to-morrow. . . . This ground's as hard as nails, for all your blankets. . . . Well, good-night, mate; I'm going to sleep."

A Run for Land

"Good-night, Moran."

Three hours later Wilbur, who had not closed his eyes, sat up and looked at Moran, sleeping quietly, her head in a pale glory of hair; looked at her, and then around him at the silent, deserted land.

"I don't know," he said to himself. "Am I a right-minded man and a thoroughbred, or a mush-head, or merely a prudent, sensible sort of chap that values his skin and bones? I'd be glad to put a name to myself." Then, more earnestly he added: "Do I love her too much, or not enough, or love her the wrong way, or how?" He leaned toward her, so close that he could catch the savor of her breath and the smell of her neck, warm with sleep. The sleeve of the coarse blue shirt was drawn up, and it seemed to him as if her bare arm, flung out at full length, had some sweet aroma of its own. Wilbur drew softly back.

"No," he said to himself decisively; "no, I guess I *am* a thoroughbred after all." It was only then that he went to sleep.

When he awoke the sea was pink with the sunrise, and one of the bay heads was all distorted and stratified by a mirage. It was hot already. Moran was sitting a few paces from him, braiding her hair.

"Hello, Moran!" he said, rousing up; "how long have you been up?"

"Since before sunrise," she said; "I've had a bath in the cove where the creek runs down. I saw a jack-rabbit."

"Seen anything of Charlie and the others?"

"They've camped on the other side of the bay. But look yonder," she added.

The junk had come in over night, and was about a mile and a half from shore.

"The deuce!" exclaimed Wilbur. "What are they after?"

"Fresh water, I guess," said Moran, knotting the end of a braid. "We'd better have breakfast in a hurry, and turn to on the *Bertha*. The tide is going out fast."

A Run for Land

While they breakfasted they kept an eye on the schooner, watching her sides and flanks as the water fell slowly away.

"Don't see anything very bad yet," said Wilbur.

"It's somewheres in her stern," remarked Moran.

In an hour's time the *Bertha Millner* was high and dry, and they could examine her at their leisure. It was Moran who found the leak.

"Pshaw!" she exclaimed, with a half-laugh, "we can stick that up in half an hour."

A single plank had started away from the stern-post; that was all. Otherwise the schooner was as sound as the day she left San Francisco. Moran and Wilbur had the damage repaired by noon, nailing the plank into its place and caulking the seams with lamp-wick. Nor could their most careful search discover any further injury.

"We're ready to go," said Moran, "so soon as she'll float. We can dig away around the bows here, make fast a line to that rock out yonder, and warp her off at next high tide. Hello! who's this?"

It was Charlie. While the two had been at work, he had come around the shore unobserved, and now stood at some little distance, smiling at them calmly.

"Well, what do you want?" cried Moran angrily. "If you had your rights, my friend, you'd be keelhauled."

"I tink um velly hot day."

"You didn't come here to say that. What do you want?"

"I come hab talkee-talk."

"We don't want to have any talkee-talk with such vermin as you. Get out!"

Charlie sat down on the beach and wiped his forehead.

"I come buy one-piecee bacon. China boy no hab got."

"We aren't selling bacon to deserters," cried Moran; "and I'll tell you this, you

filthy little monkey: Mr. Wilbur and I
are going home—back to 'Frisco—this
afternoon; and we're going to leave you
and the rest of your vipers to rot on this
beach, or to be murdered by beachcombers," and she pointed out toward the
junk. Charlie did not even follow the
direction of her gesture, and from this
very indifference Wilbur guessed that it
was precisely because of the beachcombers that the Machiavellian Chinaman had
wished to treat with his old officers.

"No hab got bacon?" he queried, lifting his eyebrows in surprise.

"Plenty; but not for you."

Charlie took a buckskin bag from his
blouse and counted out a handful of silver
and gold.

"I buy um nisi two-piecee tobacco."

"Look here," said Wilbur deliberately;
"don't you try to flim-flam us, Charlie.
We know you too well. You don't want
bacon and you don't want tobacco."

"China boy heap plenty much sick.

Two boy velly sick. I tink um die pretty soon to-molla. You catch um slop-chest; you gib me five, seven liver pill. Sabe?"

"I'll tell you what you want," cried Moran, aiming a forefinger at him, pistol fashion; "you've got a blue funk because those Kai-gingh beachcombers have come into the bay, and you're more frightened of them than you are of the schooner; and now you want us to take you home."

"How muchee?"

"A thousand dollars."

Wilbur looked at her in surprise. He had expected a refusal.

"You no hab got liver pill?" inquired Charlie blandly.

Moran turned her back on him. She and Wilbur conferred in a low voice.

"We'd better take them back, if we decently can," said Moran. "The schooner is known, of course, in Frisco. She went out with Kitchell and a crew of coolies, and she comes back with you and I aboard, and if we tell the truth about it, it will

A Run for Land

sound like a lie, and we'll have no end of trouble. Then again, can just you and I work the *Bertha* into port? In these kind of airs it's plain work, but suppose we have dirty weather? I'm not so sure."

"I gib you ten dollah fo' ten liver pill," said Charlie.

"Will you give us a thousand dollars to set you down in San Francisco?"

Charlie rose. "I go back. I tell um China boy what you say 'bout liver pill. Bime-by I come back."

"That means he'll take our offer back to his friends," said Wilbur, in a low voice. "You best hurry chop-chop," he called after Charlie; "we go home pretty soon!"

"He knows very well we can't get away before high tide to-morrow," said Moran. He'll take his time."

Later on in the afternoon Moran and Wilbur saw a small boat put off from the junk and make a landing by the creek. The beachcombers were taking on water.

The boat made three trips before evening, but the beachcombers made no show of molesting the undefended schooner, or in any way interfering with Charlie's camp on the other side of the bay.

"No!" exclaimed Moran between her teeth, as she and Wilbur were cooking supper; "no, they don't need to; they've got about a hundred and fifty thousand dollars of loot on board—*our* loot, too! Good God! it goes against the grain!"

The moon rose considerably earlier that night, and by twelve o'clock the bay was flooded with its electrical whiteness. Wilbur and Moran could plainly make out the junk tied up to the kelp off-shore. But toward one o'clock Wilbur was awakened by Moran shaking his arm.

"There's something wrong out there," she whispered; "something wrong with the junk. Hear 'em squealing? Look! look! look!" she cried of a sudden; "it's their turn now!"

Wilbur could see the crank junk, with

182

its staring red eyes, high stern and prow,
as distinctly as though at noonday. As
he watched, it seemed as if a great wave
caught her suddenly under foot. She
heaved up bodily out of the water,
dropped again with a splash, rose again,
and again fell back into her own ripples,
that, widening from her sides, broke crisp-
ly on the sand at Wilbur's feet.

Then the commotion ceased abruptly.
The bay was quiet again. An hour
passed, then two. The moon began to
set. Moran and Wilbur, wearied of
watching, had turned in again, when they
were startled to wakefulness by the creak
of oarlocks and the sound of a boat
grounding in the sand.

The coolies—the deserters from the
Bertha Millner—were there. Charlie
came forward.

"Ge' lup! Ge' lup!" he said. "Junk
all smash! Kai-gingh come ashore. I
tink him want catch um schooner."

IX

The Capture of Hoang

"WHAT smashed the junk? What wrecked her?" demanded Moran.

The deserting Chinamen huddled around Charlie, drawing close, as if finding comfort in the feel of each other's elbows.

"No can tell," answered Charlie. "Him shake, then lif' up all the same as we. Bime-by too much lif' up; him smash all to ——. Four-piecee Chinamen dlown."

"Drown! Did any of them drown?" exclaimed Moran.

"Four-piecee dlown," reiterated Charlie calmly. "One, thlee, five, nine, come asho'. Him other no come."

"Where are the ones that came ashore?" asked Wilbur.

Charlie waved a hand back into the night. "Him make um camp topside ole house."

"That old whaling-camp," prompted Moran. Then to Wilbur: "You remember—about a hundred yards north the creek?"

Wilbur, Moran, and Charlie had drawn off a little from the *Bertha Millner's* crew. The latter squatted in a line along the shore — silent, reserved, looking vaguely seaward through the night. Moran spoke again, her scowl thickening:

"What makes you think the beach-combers want our schooner?"

"Him catch um schooner sure! Him want um boat to go home. No can get."

"Let's put off to-night—right away," said Wilbur.

"Low tide," answered Moran; "and besides—Charlie, did you see them close? Were you near them?"

"No go muchee close."

"Did they have something with them,

reeved up in a hammock—something that smelled sweet?"

"Like a joss-stick, for instance?"

"No savvy; no can tell. Him try catch um schooner sure. Him velly bad China boy. See Yup China boy, velly bad. I b'long Sam Yup. Savvy?"

"Ah! the tongs?"

"Yass. I Sam Yup. Him," and he pointed to the *Bertha's* crew, "Sam Yup. All we Sam Yup; nisi him," and he waved a hand toward the beachcombers' camp; "him See Yup. Savvy?"

"It's a tong row," said Wilbur. "They're blood enemies, the See Yups and Sam Yups."

Moran fell thoughtful, digging her boot-heel into the sand, her thumbs hooked into her belt, her forehead gathered into a heavy frown. There was a silence.

"One thing," she said, at last; "we can't give up the schooner. They would take our stores as well, and then where

are we? Marooned, by Jove! How far
do you suppose we are from the nearest
town? Three hundred miles wouldn't be
a bad guess, and they've got the loot—
our ambergris—I'll swear to that. They
didn't leave that aboard when the junk
sank."

"Look here, Charlie," she said, turning
to the Chinaman. "If the beachcombers
take the schooner—the *Bertha Millner*—
from us, we'll be left to starve on this
beach."

"I tink um ya s."

"How are we going to get home? Are
you going to let them do it? Are you
going to let them have our schooner."

"I tink no can have."

"Look here," she went on, with sudden
energy. "There are only nine of them
now, to our eight. We're about even.
We can fight those swine. I know we
can. If we jumped their camp and
rushed them hard, believe me, we could
run them into the sea. Mate," she cried,

suddenly facing Wilbur, "are you game? Have you got blood in you? Those beachcombers are going to attack us to-morrow, before high tide—that's flat. There's going to be a fight anyway. We can't let them have the schooner. It's starvation for us if we do.

"They mean to make a dash for the *Bertha*, and we've got to fight them off. If there's any attacking to be done I propose to do it! I propose we jump their camp before it gets light—now—to-night—right away—run in on them there, take them by surprise, do for one or two of them if we have to, and get that ambergris. Then cut back to the schooner, up our sails, and wait for the tide to float us off. We can do it—I know we can. Mate, will you back me up?"

"Back you up? You bet I'll back you up, Moran. But——" Wilbur hesitated. "We could fight them so much more to advantage from the deck of the schooner. Why not wait for them aboard? We could have our sails up, anyhow, and we could keep the beachcombers off till the tide rose high enough to drive them back. Why not do that?"

"I tink bes' wait topside boat," assented Charlie.

"Yes; why not, Moran?"

"Because," shouted the girl, "they've got our loot. I don't propose to be plundered of $150,000 if I can help it."

"Wassa dat?" demanded Charlie. "Hunder fiftee tlousand you hab got?"

"I did have it—we had it, the mate and I. We triced a sperm whale for the beachcombers, and when they thought they had everything out of him we found a lump of ambergris in him that will weigh close to two hundred pounds. Now look here, Charlie. The beachcombers have got the stuff. It's mine— I'm going to have it back. Here's the lay. Your men can fight—you can fight yourself. We'll make it a business proposition. Help me to get that ambergris, and if we get it I'll give each one of the men $1,000, and I'll give you $1,500. You can take that up and be independent rich the rest of your life. You can chuck it and rot on this beach, for it's fight or lose the schooner; you know that as well as I do. If you've got to fight anyhow, why not fight where it's going to pay the most?"

Charlie hesitated, pursing his lips.

"How about this, Moran?" Wilbur broke forth now, unheard by Charlie. "I've just been thinking; have we got a right to this ambergris, after all? The beachcombers found the whale. It was theirs. How have we the right to take the ambergris away from them any more than the sperm and the oil and the bone? It's theirs, if you come to that. I don't know as we've the right to it."

"Darn you!" shouted Moran in a blaze of fury, "right to it, right to it! If I haven't who has? Who found it? Those dirty monkeys might have stood some show to a claim if they'd held to the one-third bargain, and offered to divy with us when they got me where I couldn't help myself. I don't say I'd give in now if they had—give in to let 'em walk off with a hundred thousand dollars that I've got as good a claim to as they have! But they've saved me the trouble of arguing the question. They've taken it all, all! and there's no bargain in the game at all now. Now the stuff belongs to the strongest of us, and I'm glad of it. They thought they were the strongest and now they're going to find out. We're dumped down here on this God-forsaken sand, and there's no law and no policemen. The strongest of us are going to live and the weakest are going to die. I'm going to live and I'm going to have my loot too, and I'm not going to split fine hairs with these robbers at this time of day. I'm going to have it all, and that's the law you're under in this case, my righteous friend!"

She turned her back upon him, spinning around upon her heel, and Wilbur felt ashamed of himself and proud of her.

"I go talkee-talk to China boy," said Charlie, coming up.

For about five minutes the Chinamen conferred together, squatting in a circle on the beach. Moran paced up and down by the stranded dory. Wilbur leaned against the bleached whale-skull, his hands in his pockets. Once he looked at his watch. It was nearly one o'clock.

"All light," said Charlie, coming out from the group at last; "him fight plenty."

"Now," exclaimed Moran, "we've no time to waste. What arms have we got?"

"We've the cutting-in spades," said Wilbur; "there's five of them. They're nearly ten feet long and the blades are as sharp as razors; you couldn't want better pikes."

"That's an idea," returned Moran, evidently willing to forget her outburst of a

moment before, perhaps already sorry for
it. The party took stock of their weapons, and five huge cutting-in spades, a
heavy knife from the galley, and a revolver of doubtful effectiveness were divided
among them. The crew took the spades,
Charlie the knife, and Wilbur the revolver. Moran had her own knife, a haft-
less dirk, such as is affected by all Norwegians, whether landsmen or sailors.
They were examining this armament and
Moran was suggesting a plan of attack,
when Hoang, the leader of the beachcombers, and one other Chinaman, appeared some little distance below them
on the beach. The moon was low and
there was no great light, but the two
beachcombers caught the flash of the points
of the spades. They halted and glanced
narrowly and suspiciously at the group.

"Beasts!" muttered Moran. "They are
up to the game—there's no surprising
them now. Talk to him Charlie; see
what he wants."

Moran of the Lady Letty

Moran, Wilbur, and Charlie came part of the way toward Hoang and his fellow, and paused some fifteen feet distant, and a long colloquy ensued. It soon became evident, however, that in reality Hoang wanted nothing of them, though with great earnestness he asserted his willingness to charter the *Bertha Millner* back to San Francisco.

"That's not his game at all," said Moran to Wilbur, in a low tone, her eyes never leaving those of the beachcomber. "He's pretty sure he could seize the *Bertha* and never pay us a stiver. They've come down to spy on us, and they're doing it, too. There's no good trying to rush their camp now. They'll go back and tell the crew that we know their lay."

It was still very dark. Near the hulk of the beached *Bertha Millner* were grouped her crew, each armed with a long and lance-like cutting-in spade, watching and listening to the conference of the chiefs. The moon, almost down, had

194

The Capture of Hoang

flushed blood-red, violently streaking the
gray, smooth surface of the bay with her
reflection. The tide was far out, rippling
quietly along the reaches of wet sand.
In the pauses of the conference the vast,
muffling silence shut down with the abruptness of a valve suddenly closed.

How it happened, just who made the
first move, in precisely what manner the
action had been planned, or what led up
to it, Wilbur could not afterward satisfac-
torily explain. There was a rush forward
—he remembered that much—a dull
thudding of feet over the resounding
beach surface, a moment's writhing struggle with a half-naked brown figure that
used knife and nail and tooth, and then
the muffling silence again, broken only
by the sound of their own panting. In
that whirl of swift action Wilbur could
reconstruct but two brief pictures: the
Chinaman, Hoang's companion, flying
like one possessed along the shore;
Hoang himself flung headlong into the

arms of the *Bertha's* coolies, and Moran,
her eyes blazing, her thick braids flying,
brandishing her fist as she shouted at the
top of her deep voice, "We've got you,
anyhow!"

They had taken Hoang prisoner,
whether by treachery or not Wilbur did
not exactly know; and, even if unfair
means had been used, he could not repress
a feeling of delight and satisfaction, as he
told himself that in the very beginning
of the fight that was to follow he and his
mates had gained the first advantage.

As the action of that night's events
became more and more accelerated, Wilbur could not but notice the change in
Moran. It was very evident that the old
Norse fighting-blood of her was all astir;
brutal, merciless, savage beyond all control. A sort of obsession seized upon her
at the near approach of battle, a frenzy of
action that was checked by nothing—
that was insensible to all restraint. At
times it was impossible for him to make

her hear him, or when she heard to understand what he was saying. Her vision contracted. It was evident that she could not see distinctly. Wilbur could no longer conceive of her as a woman of the days of civilization. She was lapsing back to the eighth century again—to the Vikings, the sea-wolves, the berserkers.

"Now you're going to talk," she cried to Hoang, as the bound Chinaman sat upon the beach, leaning his back against the great skull. "Charlie, ask him if they saved the ambergris when the junk went down — if they've got it now?" Charlie put the question in Chinese, but the beachcomber only twinkled his vicious eyes upon them and held his peace. With the full sweep of her arm, her fist clenched till the knuckles whitened, Moran struck him in the face.

"Now will you talk?" she cried. Hoang wiped the blood from his face upon his shoulder and set his jaws. He did not answer.

"You will talk before I'm done with you, my friend; don't get any wrong notions in your head about that," Moran continued, her teeth clenched. "Charlie," she added, "is there a file aboard the schooner?"

"I tink um yass, boss hab got file."

"In the tool-chest, isn't it?" Charlie nodded, and Moran ordered it to be fetched.

"If we're to fight that crowd," she said, speaking to herself and in a rapid voice, thick from excitement and passion, "we've got to know where they've hid the loot, and what weapons they've got. If they have a rifle or a shotgun with them, it's going to make a big difference for us. The other fellow escaped and has gone back to warn the rest. It's fight now, and no mistake."

The Chinaman who had been sent aboard the schooner returned, carrying a long, rather coarse-grained file. Moran took it from him.

The Capture of Hoang

"Now," she said, standing in front of Hoang, "I'll give you one more chance. Answer me. Did you bring off the ambergris, you beast, when your junk sank? Where is it now? How many men have you? What arms have you got? Have your men got a rifle! Charlie, put that all to him in your lingo, so as to make sure that he understands. Tell him if he don't talk I'm going to make him very sick."

Charlie put the questions in Chinese, pausing after each one. Hoang held his peace.

"I gave you fair warning," shouted Moran angrily, pointing at him with the file. "Will you answer?"

"Him no tell nuttin," observed Charlie.

"Fetch a cord here," commanded Moran. The cord was brought, and despite Hoang's struggles and writhings the file was thrust end-ways into his mouth and his jaws bound tightly together upon it by means of the cord passed over his head and under his chin. Some four inches of the file protruded from his lips. Moran took this end and drew it out between the beachcomber's teeth, then pushed it back slowly.

The hideous rasp of the operation turned Wilbur's blood cold within him. He looked away—out to sea, down the beach—anywhere, so that he might not see what was going forward. But the persistent grind and scrape still assaulted his ears. He turned about sharply.

"I—I—I'll go down the beach here a ways," he said quickly. "I can't stand —I'll keep watch to see if the beachcombers come up."

A few minutes later he heard Charlie hailing him.

"Chin-chin heap plenty now," said he, with a grin, as Wilbur came up.

Hoang sat on the sand in the midst of the circle. The file and coil of rope lay on the ground near by. The beachcomber was talking in a high-keyed sing-song.

but with a lisp. He told them partly in pigeon English and partly in Cantonese, which Charlie translated, that their men were eight in number, and that they had intended to seize the schooner that night, but that probably his own capture had delayed their plans. They had no rifle. A shotgun had been on board, but had gone down with the sinking of the junk. The ambergris had been cut into two lumps, and would be found in a couple of old flour-sacks in the stern of the boat in which he and his men had come ashore. They were all armed with their little hatchets. He thought two of the men carried knives as well. There was neither pistol nor revolver among them.

"It seems to me," said Wilbur, "that we've got the long end."

"We catch um boss, too!" said Charlie, pointing to Hoang.

"And we are better armed," assented Moran. "We've got the cutting-in spades."

"And the revolver, if it will shoot any farther than it will kick."

"They'll give us all the fight we want," declared Moran.

"Oh, him Kai-gingh, him fight all same devil."

"Give the men brandy, Charlie," commanded Moran. "We'll rush that camp right away."

The demijohn of spirits was brought down from the *Bertha* and passed around, Wilbur and Moran drinking from the tin cup, the coolies from the bottle. Hoang was fettered and locked in the *Bertha's* cabin.

"Now, then, are we ready?" cried Moran.

"I tink all light," answered Charlie.

The party set off down the beach. The moon had long since gone down, and the dawn was whitening over the eastern horizon. Landward, ragged blankets of morning mist lay close in the hollows here and there. It was profoundly still.

The Capture of Hoang

The stars were still out. The surface of Magdalena Bay was smooth as a sheet of gray silk.

Twenty minutes passed, half an hour, an hour. The party tramped steadily forward, Moran, Wilbur, and Charlie leading, the coolies close behind carrying the cutting-in spades over their shoulders. Slowly and in silence they made the half circuit of the bay. The *Bertha Millner* was far behind them by now, a vague gray mass in the early morning light.

"Did you ever fight before?" Moran suddenly demanded of Charlie.

"One time I fight plenty much in San Flancisco in Washington stleet. Fight-um See Yups."

Another half-hour passed. At times when they halted they began to hear the faint murmur of the creek, just beyond which was the broken and crumbling shanty, relic of an old Portuguese whaling-camp, where the beachcombers were camped. At Charlie's suggestion the

party made a circuit, describing a half
moon, to landward, so as to come out
upon the enemy sheltered by the sand-
dunes.   Twenty minutes later they
crossed the creek about four hundred
yards from the shore.   Here they spread
out into a long line, and, keeping an in-
terval of about fifteen feet between each
of them, moved cautiously forward. The
unevenness of the sand-breaks hid the
shore from view, but Moran, Wilbur, and
Charlie knew that by keeping the creek
upon their left they would come out directly upon the house.

A few moments later Charlie held up
his hand, and the men halted.   The noise
of the creek chattering into the tidewater
of the bay was plainly audible just beyond ; a ridge of sand, covered thinly with
sage-brush, and a faint column of smoke
rose into the air over the ridge itself.
They were close in.   The coolies were
halted, and, dropping upon their hands
and knees, the three leaders crawled to

the top of the break. Sheltered by a couple of sage-bushes and lying flat to the ground, Wilbur looked over and down upon the beach. The first object he made out was a crazy, roofless house, built of driftwood, the chinks plastered with 'dobe mud, the door fallen in.

Beyond, on the beach, was a flat-bottomed dingy, unpainted and foul with dirt. But all around the house the sand had been scooped and piled to form a low barricade, and behind this barricade Wilbur saw the beachcombers. There were eight of them. They were alert and ready, their hatchets in their hands. The gaze of each of them was fixed directly upon the sand-break which sheltered the *Bertha Millner's* officers and crew. They seemed to Wilbur to look him straight in the eye. They neither moved nor spoke. The silence and absolute lack of motion on the part of these small, half-naked Chinamen, with their ape-like muzzles and twinkling eyes, was ominous.

There could be no longer any doubt that the beachcombers had known of their enemies' movements and were perfectly aware of their presence behind the sand-break. Moran rose to her feet, and Wilbur and Charlie followed her example.

"There's no use hiding," she said; "they know we're here."

Charlie called up the crew. The two parties were ranged face to face. Over the eastern rim of the Pacific the blue whiteness of the early dawn was turning to a dull, roseate gold at the core of the sunrise. The headlands of Magdalena Bay stood black against the pale glow; overhead, the greater stars still shone. The monotonous, faint ripple of the creek was the only sound. It was about 3:30 o'clock.

X

A Battle

WILBUR had imagined that the fight would be hardly more than a wild rush down the slope of the beach, a dash over the beachcombers' breastworks of sand, and a brief hand-to-hand scrimmage around the old cabin. In all accounts he had ever read of such affairs, and in all ideas he had entertained on the subject, this had always been the case. The two bodies had shocked together like a college rush, there had been five minutes' play of knife and club and gun, a confused whirl of dust and smoke, and all was over before one had time either to think or be afraid. But nothing of the kind happened that morning.

The *Bertha Millner's* crew, in a long line, Moran at one end, Wilbur at the other, and Charlie in the centre, came on toward the beachcombers, step by step. There was little outcry. Each contestant singled out his enemy, and made slowly for him with eyes fixed and weapon ready, regardless of the movements of his mates.

"See any rifles among them, Charlie?" shouted Moran, suddenly breaking the silence.

"No, I tink no hab got," answered Charlie.

Wilbur took another step forward and cocked his revolver. One of the beach-combers shouted out something in angry vernacular, and Charlie instantly respond-ed. All this time the line had been slowly advancing upon the enemy, and Wilbur began to wonder how long that heartbreaking suspense was to continue. This was not at all what he had im-agined. Already he was within twenty feet of his man, could see the evil glint of his slant, small eye, and the shine of

208

A Battle

his yellow body, naked to the belt. Still foot by foot the forward movement continued. The Chinese on either side had begun exchanging insults; the still, hot air of the tropic dawn was vibrant with the Cantonese monosyllables tossed back and forth like tennis-balls over the low sand rampart. The thing was degenerating into a farce—the *Bertha's* Chinamen would not fight.

Back there, under the shelter of the schooner, it was all very well to talk, and they had been very brave when they had all flung themselves upon Hoang. Here, face to face with the enemy, the sun striking off heliograph flashes from their knives and spades, it was a vastly different matter. The thing, to Wilbur's mind, should have been done suddenly if it was to be done at all. The best course now was to return to camp and try some other plan. Charlie shouted a direction to him in pigeon English that he did not understand, but he answered all right,

14   209

and moved forward another step so as to be in line with the coolie at his left.

The liquor that he had drunk before starting began suddenly to affect him, yet he knew that his head was yet clear. He could not bring himself to run away before them all, but he would have given much to have discovered a good reason for postponing the fight—if fight there was to be.

He remembered the cocked revolver in his hand, and, suddenly raising it, fired point-blank at his man, not fifteen feet away. The hammer snapped on the nipple, but the cartridge did not explode. Wilbur turned to the Chinaman next him in line, exclaiming excitedly:

"Here, say, have you got a knife—something I can fight with? This gun's no good."

There was a shout from Moran:

"Look out, here they come!"

Two of the beachcombers suddenly sprang over the sand breastworks and ran toward Charlie, their knives held low in front of them, ready to rip.

"Shoot! shoot! shoot!" shouted Moran rapidly.

Wilbur's revolver was a self-cocker. He raised it again, drawing hard on the trigger as he did so. It roared and leaped in his hand, and a whiff of burnt powder came to his nostrils. Then Wilbur was astonished to hear himself shout at the top of his voice:

"Come on now, get into them—get into them now, everybody!"

The *Bertha's* Chinamen were all running forward, three of them well in advance of the others. In the rear Charlie was at grapples with a beachcomber who fought with a knife in each hand, and Wilbur had a sudden glimpse of another sitting on the sand with his hand to his mouth, the blood spurting between his fingers.

Wilbur suddenly realized that he held a knife, and that he was directly abreast the sand rampart. How he got the knife

he could not tell, though he afterward
distinctly remembered throwing away his
revolver, loaded as it was. He had
leaped the breastworks, he knew that,
and between him and the vast bright blur
of the ocean he saw one of the beachcombers backing away and watching him
intently, his hatchet in his hand. Wilbur
had only time to think that he himself
would no doubt be killed within the next
few moments, when this latter halted
abruptly, took a step forward, and, instead
of striking downward, as Wilbur had an-
ticipated, dropped upon his knee and
struck with all his might at the calf of
Wilbur's leg. It was only the thickness
of his boots that saved Wilbur from being hamstrung where he stood. As it
was, he felt the blade bite almost to the
bone, and heard the blood squelch in the
sole of his boot, as he staggered for the
moment, almost tripping over the man in
front of him.

The Chinaman sprang to his feet again,

A Battle

but Wilbur was at him in an instant, feeling instinctively that his chance was to close with his man, and so bring his own superior weight and strength to bear. Again and again he tried to run in and grip the slim yellow body, but the other dodged and backed away, as hard to hold as any fish. All around and back of him now Wilbur heard the hideous sound of stamping and struggling, and the noise of hoarse, quick shouts and the rebound of bodies falling and rolling upon the hard, smooth beach. The thing had not been a farce, after all. This was fighting at last, and there within arm's length were men grappling and gripping and hitting one another, each honestly striving to kill his fellow—Chinamen all, fighting in barbarous Oriental fashion with nails and teeth when the knife or hatchet failed. What did he, clubman and collegeman, in that hideous trouble that wrought itself out there on that heat-stricken tropic beach under that morning's sun?

Suddenly there was a flash of red flame, and a billow of thick, yellow smoke filled all the air. The cabin was afire. The hatchet-man with whom Wilbur was fighting had been backing in this direction. He was close in when the fire began to leap from the one window; now he could go no farther. He turned to run sideways between his enemy and the burning cabin. Wilbur thrust his foot sharply forward; the beachcomber tripped, staggered, and before he had reached the ground Wilbur had driven home the knife.

Then suddenly, at the sight of his smitten enemy rolling on the ground at his feet, the primitive man, the half-brute of the stone age, leaped to life in Wilbur's breast—he felt his muscles thrilling with a strength they had not known before. His nerves, stretched tense as harp-strings, were vibrating to a new tune. His blood spun through his veins till his ears roared with the rush of

214

A Battle

it. Never nad he conceived of such
savage exultation as that which mastered
him at that instant. The knowledge
that he could kill filled him with a sense
of power that was veritably royal. He
felt physically larger. It was the joy of
battle, the horrid exhilaration of killing,
the animal of the race, the human brute
suddenly aroused and dominating every
instinct and tradition of centuries of civilization. The fight still was going forward.

Wilbur could hear the sounds of it,
though from where he stood all sight was
shut off by the smoke of the burning
house. As he turned about, knife in
hand, debating what next he should do,
a figure burst down upon him, shadowy
and distorted through the haze.

It was Moran, but Moran as Wilbur
had never seen her before. Her eyes
were blazing under her thick frown like
fire under a bush. Her arms were bared
to the elbow, her heavy ropes of hair fly-

ing and coiling from her in all direc-
tions, while with a voice hoarse from
shouting she sang, or rather chanted, in
her long-forgotten Norse tongue, frag-
ments of old sagas, words, and sentences,
meaningless even to herself. The fury
of battle had exalted her to a sort of
frenzy. She was beside herself with excitement. Once more she had lapsed
back to the Vikings and sea-rovers of the
tenth century—she was Brunhilde again,
a shield-maiden, a Valkyrie, a bersirker
and the daughter of bersirkers, and like
them she fought in a veritable frenzy,
seeing nothing, hearing nothing, every
sense exalted, every force doubled, insensible to pain, deaf to all reason.

Her dirk uplifted, she rushed upon
Wilbur, never once pausing in her chant.
Wilbur shouted a warning to her as she
came on, puzzled beyond words, startled
back to a consciousness of himself again
by this insensate attack.

"Moran! Moran!" he called. "What

A Battle

is it—you're wrong! It's I. It's Wilbur—your mate, can't you see?"

Moran could not see—blind to friend
or foe, as she was deaf to reason, she
struck at him with all the strength of
her arm. But there was no skill in her
fighting now. Wilbur dropped his own
knife and gripped her right wrist. She
closed with him upon the instant, clutch-
ing at his throat with her one free hand;
and as he felt her strength—doubled and
tripled in the fury of her madness—Wilbur knew that, however easily he had
overcome his enemy of a moment before,
he was now fighting for his very life.

At first, Wilbur merely struggled to
keep her from him—to prevent her using
her dirk. He tried not to hurt her. But
what with the spirits he had drunk before the attack, what with the excitement
of the attack itself and the sudden un-
leashing of the brute in him an instant
before, the whole affair grew dim and
hazy in his mind. He ceased to see

things in their proportion. His new-
found strength gloried in matching itself
with another strength that was its equal.
He fought with Moran—not as he would
fight with either woman or man, or with
anything human, for the matter of that.
He fought with her as against some im-
personal force that it was incumbent upon
him to conquer—that it was imperative
he should conquer if he wished to live.
When she struck, he struck blow for
blow, force for force, his strength against
hers, glorying in that strange contest,
though he never once forgot that this last
enemy was the girl he loved. It was not
Moran whom he fought; it was her force,
her determination, her will, her splendid
independence, that he set himself to conquer.

Already she had dropped or flung away
the dirk, and their battle had become an
issue of sheer physical strength between
them. It was a question now as to who
should master the other. Twice she had

fought Wilbur to his knees, the heel of
her hand upon his face, his head thrust
back between his shoulders, and twice he
had wrenched away, rising to his feet
again, panting, bleeding even, but with
his teeth set and all his resolution at the
sticking-point.   Once he saw his chance,
and planted his knuckles squarely between her eyes where her frown was
knotted hard, hoping to stun her and end
the fight once and for all.   But the blow
did not seem to affect her in the least.
By this time he saw that her bersirker
rage had worked itself clear as ferment-
ing wine clears itself, and that she knew
now with whom she was fighting; and
he seemed now to understand the incom-
prehensible, and to sympathize with her
joy in measuring her strength against
his; and yet he knew that the combat
was deadly serious, and that more than
life was at stake.   Moran despised a
weakling.

For an instant, as they fell apart, she

stood off, breathing hard and rolling up her sleeve; then, as she started forward again, Wilbur met her half-way, caught her round the neck and under the arm, gripping her left wrist with his right hand behind her; then, exerting every ounce of strength he yet retained, he thrust her down and from him, until at length, using his hip as a pivot, he swung her off her feet, threw her fairly on her back, and held her so, one knee upon her chest, his hands closed vise-like on her wrists.

Then suddenly Moran gave up, relaxing in his grasp all in a second, and, to his great surprise, suddenly smiled.

"Ho! mate," she exclaimed; "that was a tough one; but I'm beaten— you're stronger than I thought for."

Wilbur released her and rose to his feet.

"Here," she continued, "give me your hand. I'm as weak as a kitten." As Wilbur helped her to her feet, she put her

A Battle

hand to her forehead, where his knuckles
had left their mark, and frowned at him,
but not ill-naturedly.

"Next time you do that," she said,
"use a rock or a belaying-pin, or something
that won't hurt—not your fist, mate."
She looked at him admiringly. "What a
two-fisted, brawny dray-horse it is! I
told you I was stronger than most men,
didn't I? But I'm the weaker of us two,
and that's a fact. You've beaten, mate—
I admit it; you've conquered me, and,"
she continued, smiling again and shaking
him by the shoulder,—"and, mate, do you
know, I love you for it."

XI

A Change in Leaders

"WELL," exclaimed Wilbur at length, the excitement of the fight returning upon him. "We have plenty to do yet. Come on, Moran."

It was no longer Moran who took the initiative—who was the leader. The brief fight upon the shore had changed all that. It was Wilbur who was now the master, it was Wilbur who was aggressive. He had known what it meant to kill. He was no longer afraid of anything, no longer hesitating. He had felt a sudden quadrupling of all his strength, moral and physical.

All that was strong and virile and brutal in him seemed to harden and stiffen in the moment after he had seen

the beachcomber collapse limply on the
sand under that last strong knife-blow;
and a sense of triumph, of boundless self-
confidence, leaped within him, so that he
shouted aloud in a very excess of exhilaration; and snatching up a heavy cutting-in spade, that had been dropped in
the fight near the burning cabin, tossed it
high into the air, catching it again as it
descended, like any exultant savage.

"Come on!" he cried to **Moran**;
"where are the beachcombers gone? I'm
going to get one more before the show is
over."

The two passed out of the zone of
smoke, and reached the other side of the
burning cabin just in time to see the last
of the struggle. The whole affair had
not taken more than a quarter of an
hour. In the end the beachcombers had
been beaten. Four had fled into the
waste of sand and sage that lay back of
the shore, and had not been pursued. A
fifth had been almost hamstrung by one

of the *Bertha's* coolies, and had given himself up. A sixth, squealing and shriek-
ing like a tiger-cat, had been made prisoner; and Wilbur himself had accounted
for the seventh.

As Wilbur and Moran came around
the cabin they saw the *Bertha Millner's*
Chinamen in a group, not far from the
water's edge, reassembled after the fight—
panting and bloody, some of them bare
to the belt, their weapons still in their
hands. Here and there was a bandaged
arm or head; but their number was complete—or no, was it complete?

"Ought to be one more," said Wilbur,
anxiously hastening forward.

As the two came up the coolies parted,
and Wilbur saw one of them, his head
propped upon a rolled-up blouse, lying
ominously still on the trampled sand.

"It's Charlie!" exclaimed Moran.

"Where's he hurt?" cried Wilbur to
the group of coolies. "Jim!—where's
Jim? Where's he hurt, Jim?"

A Change in Leaders

Jim, the only member of the crew besides Charlie who could understand or speak English, answered:

"Kai-gingh him fin' pistol, you' pistol; Charlie him fight plenty; bimeby, when he no see, one-piecee Kai-gingh he come up behin', shoot um Charlie in side,— savvy?"

"Did he kill him? Is he dead?"

"No, I tinkum die plenty soon; him no savvy nuttin' now, him all-same sleep. Plenty soon bimeby him sleep for good, I tink."

There was little blood to be seen when Wilbur gently unwrapped the torn sleeve of a blouse that had been used as a bandage. Just under the armpit was the mark of the bullet—a small puncture already closed, half hidden under a clot or two of blood. The coolie lay quite unconscious, his eyes wide open, drawing a faint, quick breath at irregular intervals.

"What do you think, mate?" asked Moran in a low voice.

"I think he's got it through the lungs," answered Wilbur, frowning in distress and perplexity. "Poor old Charlie!"

Moran went down on a knee, and put a finger on the slim, corded wrist, yellow as old ivory.

"Charlie," she called,—"Charlie, here, don't you know me? Wake up, old chap! It's Moran. You're not hurt so very bad, are you?"

Charlie's eyes closed and opened a couple of times.

"No can tell," he answered feebly; "hurt plenty big"; then he began to cough.

Wilbur drew a sigh of relief. "He's all right!" he exclaimed.

"Yes, I think he's all right," assented Moran.

"First thing to do now is to get him aboard the schooner," said Wilbur. "We'll take him right across in the beachcombers' dory here. By Jove!" he exclaimed on a sudden. "The ambergris —I'd forgotten all about it." His heart

sank. In the hideous confusion of that
morning's work, all thought of the loot
had been forgotten. Had the battle
been for nothing, after all? The moment the beachcombers had been made
aware of the meditated attack, it would
have been an easy matter for them to
have hidden the ambergris—destroyed
it even.

In two strides Wilbur had reached the
beachcombers' dory and was groping in
the forward cuddy. Then he uttered a
great shout of satisfaction. The "stuff"
was there, all of it, though the mass had
been cut into quarters, three parts of it
stowed in tea-flails, the fourth still reeved
up in the hammock netting.

"We've got it!" he cried to Moran,
who had followed him. "We've got it,
Moran! Over $100,000. We're rich—
rich as boodlers, you and I. Oh, it was
worth fighting for, after all, wasn't it?
Now we'll get out of here,—now we'll cut
for home."

Moran of the Lady Letty

"It's only Charlie I'm thinking about," answered Moran, hesitating. "If it wasn't for that we'd be all right. I don't know whether we did right, after all, in jumping the camp here. I wouldn't like to feel that I'd got Charlie into our quarrel only to have him killed."

Wilbur stared at this new Moran in no little amazement. Where was the reckless, untamed girl of the previous night, who had sworn at him and denounced his niggling misgivings as to right and wrong?

"Hoh!" he retorted impatiently, "Charlie's right enough. And, besides, I didn't force him to anything. I—we, that is, we took the same chances. If I hadn't done for my man there behind the cabin, he would have done for me. At all events, we carried our point. We got the loot. They took it from us, and we were strong enough to get it back."

Moran merely nodded, as though satisfied with his decision, and added:

A Change in Leaders

"Well, what next, mate?"

"We'll get back to the *Bertha* now and put to sea as soon as we can catch the tide. I'll send Jim and two of the other men across in the dory with Charlie. The rest of us will go around by the shore. We've got to have a chin-chin with Hoang, if he don't get loose aboard there and fire the boat before we can get back. I don't propose taking these beachcombers back to Frisco with us."

"What will we do with the two prisoners?" she asked.

"Let them go; we've got their arms."

The positions of the two were reversed. It was Wilbur who assumed control and direction of what went forward, Moran taking his advice and relying upon his judgment.

In accordance with Wilbur's orders, Charlie was carried aboard the dory, which, with two Chinamen at the oars, and the ambergris stowed again into the

cuddy, at once set off for the schooner.
Wilbur himself cut the ropes on the two
prisoners, and bade them shift for themselves. The rest of the party returned
to the *Bertha Millner* around the wide
sweep of the beach.

It was only by high noon, under the
flogging of a merciless sun, that the entire crew of the little schooner once more
reassembled under the shadow of her
stranded hulk. They were quite worn
out; and as soon as Charlie was lifted
aboard, and the ambergris—or, as they
spoke of it now, the "loot"—was safely
stowed in the cabin, Wilbur allowed the
Chinamen three or four hours' rest.
They had had neither breakfast nor dinner; but their exhaustion was greater
than their hunger, and in a few moments
the entire half-dozen were stretched out
asleep on the forward deck in the shadow
of the foresail, raised for the purpose of
sheltering them. However, Wilbur and
Moran sought out Hoang, whom they

found as they had left him—bound upon
the floor of the cabin.

"Now we have a talk—savvy?" Wilbur told him as he loosed the ropes about
his wrists and ankles. "We got our loot
back from you, old man, and we got one
of your men into the bargain. You woke
up the wrong crowd, Hoang, when you
went up against this outfit. You're in
a bad way, my friend. Your junk is
wrecked; all your oil and blubber from
the whale is lost; four of your men have
run away, one is killed, another one we
caught and let go, another one has been
hamstrung; and you yourself are our
prisoner, with your teeth filed down to
your gums. Now," continued Wilbur,
with the profoundest gravity, "I hope
this will be a lesson to you. Don't try
and get too much the next time. Just
be content with what is yours by right,
or what you are strong enough to keep,
and don't try to fight white people.
Other coolies, I don't say. But when you

try to get the better of white people you are out of your class."

The little beachcomber (he was scarcely above five feet) rubbed his chafed wrists, and fixed Wilbur with his tiny, twinkling eyes.

" What you do now?"

" We go home. I'm going to maroon you and your people here on this beach. You deserve that I should let you eat your fists by way of table-board; but I'm no such dirt as you. When our men left the schooner they brought off with them a good share of our provisions. I'll leave them here for you—and there's plenty of turtle and abalone to be had for the catching. Some of the American men-of-war, I believe, come down to this bay for target-practice twice a year, and if we speak any on the way up we'll ask them to call here for castaways. That's what I'll do for you, and that's all! If you don't like it, you can set out to march up the coast till you hit a town; but I wouldn't advise you

to try it. Now what have you got to
say?"

Hoang was silent. His queue had become unbound for half its length, and he
plaited it anew, winking his eyes thoughtfully.

"Well, what do you say?" said Moran.

"I lose face," answered Hoang at length,
calmly.

"You lose face? What do you mean?"

"I lose face," he insisted; then added: "I heap 'shamed. You fightee my
China boy, you catchee me. My boy no
mo' hab me fo' boss—savvy? I go back,
him no likee me. Mebbee all same killee
me. I lose face—no mo' boss."

"What a herd of wild cattle!" muttered
Wilbur.

"There's something in what he says,
don't you think, mate?" observed Moran,
bringing a braid over each shoulder and
stroking it according to her habit.

"We'll ask Jim about it," decided Wilbur.

But Jim at once confirmed Hoang's statement. "Oh, Kai-gingh killum no-good boss, fo' sure," he declared.

"Don't you think, mate," said **Moran**, "we'd better take him up to 'Frisco with us? We've had enough fighting and killing."

So it was arranged that the defeated beachcomber, the whipped buccaneer, who had "lost face" and no longer dared look his men in the eye, should be taken aboard.

By four o'clock next morning Wilbur had the hands at work digging the sand from around the *Bertha Millner's* bow. The line by which she was to be warped off was run out to the ledge of the rock; fresh water was taken on; provisions for the marooned beachcombers were cached upon the beach; the dory was taken aboard, gaskets were cast off, and hatches battened down.

At high tide, all hands straining upon the warp, the schooner was floated off, and under touch of the lightest airs drew

almost imperceptibly away from the land.
They were quite an hour crawling out
to the heads of the bay. But here the
breeze was freshening. Moran took the
wheel; the flying-jib and staysail were
set; the wake began to whiten under the
schooner's stern, the forefoot sang; the
Pacific opened out more and more; and by
12:30 o'clock Moran put the wheel over,
and, as the schooner's bow swung to the
northward, cried to Wilbur:

"Mate, look your last of Magdalena
Bay!"

Standing at her side, Wilbur turned
and swept the curve of the coast with a
single glance. The vast, heat-scourged
hoop of yellow sand, the still, smooth
shield of indigo water, with its beds of
kelp, had become insensibly dear to him.
It was all familiar, friendly, and hospi-
table. Hardly an acre of that sweep of
beach that did not hold the impress of
his foot. There was the point near by
the creek where he and Moran first land-

ed to fill the water-casks and to gather
abalones; the creek itself, where he
had snared quail; the sand-spit, with its
whitened whale's skull, where he and
Moran had beached the schooner; and
there, last of all, that spot of black over
which still hung a haze of brown gray
smoke, the charred ruins of the old Portuguese whaling-cabin, where they had
outfought the beachcombers.

For a moment Wilbur and Moran
looked back without speaking. They
stood on the quarter-deck, in the shadow
of the mainsail, shut off from the sight of
the schooner's crew, and for the instant
quite alone.

"Well, Moran, it's good-by to the old
place, isn't it?" said Wilbur at length.

"Yes," she said, her deep voice pitched
even deeper than usual. "Mate, great
things have happened there."

"It doesn't look like a place for a tong
row with Chinese pirates, though, does
it?" he said; but even as he spoke the

words, he guessed that that was not what
he meant.

"Oh, what did that amount to?" she
said, with an impatient movement of her
head. "It was there that I first knew
myself; and knew that, after all, you were
a man and I was a woman; and that
there was just us—you and I—in the
world; and that you loved me and I
loved you, and that nothing else was
worth thinking of."

Wilbur shut his hand down over hers
as it gripped a spoke of the wheel.

"Moran, I knew that long since," he
said. "Such a month as this has been!
Why, I feel as though I had only begun
to live since I began to love you."

"And you do, mate?" she answered,—
"you do love me, and always will? Oh!
you don't know," she went on, interrupt-
ing his answer, "you haven't a guess,
how the last two days have changed me.
Something has happened here,"—and she
put both her hands over her breast. "I'm

all different here, mate. It's all you inside here—all you! And it hurts, and
I'm proud that it does hurt. Oh!" she
cried, of a sudden, "I don't know how to
love yet, and I do it very badly, and I
can't tell you how I feel, because I can't
even tell it to myself. But you must be
good to me now." The deep voice trembled a little. "Good to me, mate, and
true to me, mate, because I've only you,
and all of me is yours. Mate, be good to
me, and always be kind to me. I'm not
Moran any more. I'm not proud and
strong and independent, and I don't want
to be lonely. I want you—I want you
always with me. I'm just a woman now,
dear—just a woman that loves you with a
heart she's just found."

Wilbur could find no words to answer.
There was something so pathetic and at
the same time so noble in Moran's complete surrender of herself, and her depen-
dence upon him, her unquestioned trust
in him and his goodness, that he was sud-

denly smitten with awe at the sacredness
of the obligation thus imposed on him.
She was his now, to have and to hold, to
keep, to protect, and to defend—she who
was once so glorious of her strength, of
her savage isolation, her unviolate, pris-
tine maidenhood. All words seemed fu-
tile and inadequate to him.

She came close to him, and put her
hands upon his shoulders, and, looking
him squarely in the eye, said:

"You do love me, mate, and you always will?"

"Always, Moran," said Wilbur, simply.
He took her in his arms, and she laid her
cheek against his for a moment, then took
his head between her hands and kissed
him.

Two days passed. The *Bertha Millner*
held steadily to her northward course,
Moran keeping her well in toward the
land. Wilbur maintained a lookout from
the crow's-nest in the hope of sighting
some white cruiser or battleship on her

way south for target-practice. In the cache of provisions he had left for the beachcombers he had inserted a message, written by Hoang, to the effect that they might expect to be taken off by a United States man-of-war within the month.

Hoang did not readily recover his "loss of face." The *Bertha's* Chinamen would have nothing to do with this member of a hostile tong; and the humiliated beach-comber kept almost entirely to himself, sitting on the forecastle-head all day long, smoking his sui-yen-hu and brooding silently to himself.

Moran had taken the lump of ambergris from out Kitchell's old hammock, and had slung the hammock itself in the schooner's waist, and Charlie was made as comfort-able as possible therein. They could do but little for him, however; and he was taken from time to time with spells of coughing that racked him with a dreadful agony. At length one noon, just after Moran had taken the sun and had cal-

A Change in Leaders

culated that the *Bertha* was some eight
miles to the southwest of San Diego, she
was surprised to hear Wilbur calling her
sharply. She ran to him, and found him
standing in the waist by Charlie's hammock.

The Chinaman was dying, and knew it.
He was talking in a faint and feeble voice
to Wilbur as she came up, and was trying
to explain to him that he was sorry he
had deserted the schooner during the scare
in the bay.

"Plenty muchee solly," he said; "China
boy, him heap flaid of Feng-shui. When
Feng-shui no likee, we then must go
chop-chop. Plenty much solly I leaveum schooner that night; solly plenty—
savvy?"

"Of course we savvy, Charlie," said
Moran. "You weren't afraid when it
came to fighting."

"I die pletty soon," said Charlie calmly. "You say you gib me fifteen hundled
dollah?"

" Yes, yes; that was our promise. What do you want done with it, Charlie?"

" I want plenty fine funeral in China-town in San Flancisco. Oh, heap fine! You buy um first-chop coffin—savvy? Silver heap much—costum big money. You gib my money to Hop Sing Associa-tion, topside Ming Yen temple. You savvy Hop Sing?—one Six Companies."

" Yes, yes."

" Tellum Hop Sing I want funeral— four-piecee horse. You no flogettee horse?" he added apprehensively.

" No, I'll not forget the horses, Charlie. You shall have four."

" Want six-piecee band musicians— China music—heap plenty gong. You no flogettee? Two-piecee priest, all dressum white—savvy? You mus' buyum coffin yo'self. Velly fine coffin, heap much sil-ver, an' four-piecee horse. You catchum fireclacker—one, five, seven hundled fire-clacker, makeum big noise; an' loast pig, an' plenty lice an' China blandy. Heap

fine funeral, costum fifteen hundled dollah. I be bury all same Mandarin—all
same Little Pete. You plomise, sure?"

"I promise you, Charlie. You shall
have a funeral finer than Little Pete's."

Charlie nodded his head contentedly,
drawing a breath of satisfaction.

"Bimeby Hop Sing sendum body back
China." He closed his eyes and lay for
a long time, worn out with the effort
of speaking, as if asleep. Suddenly he
opened his eyes wide. "You no flogettee
horse?"

"Four horses, Charlie. I'll remember."

He drooped once more, only to rouse
again at the end of a few minutes with:

"First-chop coffin, plenty much silver";
and again, a little later and very feebly:
"Six-piecee—band music—China music;
—four-piecee—gong—four."

"I promise you, Charlie," said Wilbur.

"Now," answered Charlie,—"now I
die."

And the low-caste Cantonese coolie,

with all the dignity and calmness of a Cicero, composed himself for death.

An hour later Wilbur and Moran knew that he was dead. Yet, though they had never left the hammock, they could not have told at just what moment he died.

Later, on that same afternoon, Wilbur, from the crow's-nest, saw the lighthouse on Point Loma and the huge rambling bulk of the Coronado Hotel spreading out and along the beach.

It was the outpost of civilization. They were getting back to the world again. Within an hour's ride of the hotel were San Diego, railroads, newspapers, and policemen. Just off the hotel, however, Wilbur could discern the gleaming white hull of a United States man-of-war. With the glass he could make her out to be one of the monitors—the *Monterey* in all probability.

After advising with Moran, it was decided to put in to land. The report as to the castaways could be made to the *Mon-*

terey, and Charlie's body forwarded to his tong in San Francisco.

In two hours' time the schooner was well up, and Wilbur stood by Moran's side at the wheel, watching and studying the familiar aspect of Coronado Beach.

" It's a great winter resort," he told her. " I was down here with a party two years ago. Nothing has changed. You see that big sort of round wing, Moran, all full of windows? That's the dining-room. And there's the bathhouse and the bowling-alley. See the people on the beach, and the girls in white duck skirts; and look up there by the veranda—let me take the glass—yes, there's a tally-ho coach. Isn't it queer to get back to this sort of thing after Magdalena Bay and the beachcombers?"

Moran spun the wheel without reply, and gave an order to Jim to ease off the foresheet.

XII

New Conditions

THE winter season at the Hotel del Coronado had been unusually gay that year, and the young lady who wrote the society news in diary form for one of the San Francisco weekly papers had held forth at much length upon the hotel's "unbroken succession of festivities." She had also noted that "prominent among the newest arrivals" had been Mr. Nat Ridgeway, of San Francisco, who had brought down from the city, aboard his elegant and sumptuously fitted yacht *Petrel*, a jolly party, composed largely of the season's débutantes. To be mentioned in the latter category was Miss Josie Herrick, whose lavender coming-out tea at the beginning of the season was still a subject of comment among the gossips — and all the rest of it.

The *Petrel* had been in the harbor but a few days, and on this evening a dance was given at the hotel in honor of her arrival. It was to be a cotillon, and Nat Ridgeway was going to lead with Josie Herrick. There had been a coaching party to Tia Juana that day, and Miss Herrick had returned to the hotel only in time to dress. By 9:30 she emerged from the process--which had involved her mother, her younger sister, her maid, and one of the hotel chambermaids—a dainty, firm-corseted little body, all tulle, white satin, and high-piled hair. She carried Maréchal Niel roses, ordered by wire from Monterey; and about an hour later, when Ridgeway gave the nod to the waiting musicians, and swung her off to the beat of a two-step, there was not a more graceful little figure upon the floor of the incomparable round ballroom of the Coronado Hotel.

Moran of the Lady Letty

The cotillon was a great success. The ensigns and younger officers of the monitor—at that time anchored off the hotel—attended in uniform; and enough of the members of what was known in San Francisco as the "dancing set" were present to give the affair the necessary entrain. Even Jerry Haight, who belonged more distinctly to the "country-club set," and who had spent the early part of that winter shooting elk in Oregon, was among the ranks of the "rovers," who grouped themselves about the draughty doorways, and endeavored to appear unconscious each time Ridgeway gave the signal for a "break."

The figures had gone round the hall once. The "first set" was out again, and as Ridgeway guided Miss Herrick by the "rovers" she looked over the array of shirt-fronts, searching for Jerry Haight.

"Do you see Mr. Haight?" she asked of Ridgeway. "I wanted to favor him this break. I owe him two already, and he'll never forgive me if I overlook him now."

Jerry Haight had gone to the hotel office for a few moments' rest and a cigarette, and was nowhere in sight. But when the set broke, and Miss Herrick, despairing of Jerry, had started out to favor one of the younger ensigns, she suddenly jostled against him, pushing his way eagerly across the floor in the direction of the musicians' platform.

"Oh!" she cried, "Mr. Haight, you've missed your chance—I've been looking for you."

But Jerry did not hear—he seemed very excited. He crossed the floor, almost running, and went up on the platform where the musicians were meandering softly through the mazes of "La Paloma," and brought them to an abrupt silence.

"Here, I say, Haight!" exclaimed Ridgeway, who was near by, "you can't break up my figure like that."

"Gi' me a call there on the bugle,"

said Haight rapidly to the cornetist. "Anything to make 'em keep quiet a moment."

The cornetist sounded a couple of notes, and the cotillon paused in the very act of the break. The shuffling of feet grew still, and the conversation ceased. A diamond brooch had been found, no doubt, or some supper announcement was to be made. But Jerry Haight, with a great sweep of his arm, the forgotten cigarette between his fingers, shouted out breathlessly :

" Ross Wilbur is out in the office of the hotel !"

There was an instant's silence, and then a great shout. Wilbur found ! Ross Wilbur come back from the dead ! Ross Wilbur, hunted for and bootlessly traced from Buenos Ayres in the south to the Aleutian Islands in the north. Ross Wilbur, the puzzle of every detective bureau on the coast; the subject of a thousand theories; whose name had figured in the scareheads of every newspaper west of the

Mississippi. Ross Wilbur, seen at a fashionable tea and his club of an afternoon, then suddenly blotted out from the world of men; swallowed up and engulfed by the unknown, with not so much as a button left behind. Ross Wilbur the suicide; Ross Wilbur the murdered; Ross Wilbur, victim of a band of kidnappers, the hero of some dreadful story that was never to be told, the mystery, the legend, — behold he was there! Back from the unknown, dropped from the clouds, spewed up again from the bowels of the earth—a veritable god from the machine who in a single instant was to disentangle all the unexplained complications of those past winter months.

"Here he comes!" shouted Jerry, his eyes caught by a group of men in full dress and gold lace who came tramping down the hall to the ballroom, bearing a nondescript figure on their shoulders. "Here he comes—the boys are bringing him in here! Oh!" he cried, turning to the musicians,

"can't you play something?—anything!
Hit it up for all you're worth! Ridgeway
—Nat, look here! Ross was Yale, y'
know—Yale '95; ain't we enough Yale
men here to give him the yell?"

Out of all time and tune, but with a
vigor that made up for both, the musicians banged into a patriotic air. Jerry,
standing on a chair that itself was standing on the platform, led half-a-dozen fran-
tic men in the long thunder of the "Brek-
kek-kek-kex, co-ex, co-ex."

Around the edges of the hall excited
girls, and chaperons themselves no less
agitated, were standing up on chairs and
benches, splitting their gloves and breaking their fans in their enthusiasm; while
every male dancer on the floor—ensigns in
their gold-faced uniforms and "rovers"
in starched and immaculate shirt-bosoms
—cheered and cheered and struggled with
one another to shake hands with a man
whom two of their number—old Yale
grads., with memories of athletic triumphs

yet in their minds—carried into that ball-room, borne high upon their shoulders.

And the hero of the occasion, the centre of all this enthusiasm—thus carried as if in triumph into this assembly in evening dress, in white tulle and whiter kid, odor-ous of delicate sachets and scarce-percep-tible perfumes—was a figure unhandsome and unkempt beyond description. His hair was long, and hanging over his eyes. A thick, uncared-for beard concealed the mouth and chin. He was dressed in a Chinaman's blouse and jeans—the latter thrust into slashed and tattered boots. The tan and weatherbeatings of nearly half a year of the tropics were spread over his face; a partly healed scar disfigured one temple and cheek-bone; the hands, to the very finger-nails, were gray with grime; the jeans and blouse and boots were fouled with grease, with oil, with pitch, and all manner of the dirt of an un-cared-for ship. And as the dancers of the cotillon pressed about, and a hundred kid-gloved hands stretched toward his own palms, there fell from Wilbur's belt upon the waxed floor of the ballroom the knife he had so grimly used in the fight upon the beach, the ugly stains still blackening on the haft.

There was no more cotillon that night. They put him down at last; and in half-a-dozen sentences Wilbur told them of how he had been shanghaied—told them of Magdalena Bay, his fortune in the ambergris, and the fight with the beachcombers.

"You people are going down there for target-practice, aren't you?" he said, turning to one of the *Monterey's* officers in the crowd about him. "Yes? Well, you'll find the coolies there, on the beach, waiting for you. All but one," he added, grimly.

"We marooned six of them, but the seventh didn't need to be marooned. They tried to plunder us of our boat, but by ——, we made it interesting for 'em!"

"I say, steady, old man!" exclaimed

Nat Ridgeway, glancing nervously toward
the girls in the surrounding group. "This
isn't Magdalena Bay, you know."

And for the first time Wilbur felt a
genuine pang of disappointment and regret
as he realized that it was not.

Half an hour later, Ridgeway drew him
aside. "I say, Ross, let's get out of here.
You can't stand here talking all night.
Jerry and you and I will go up to my
rooms, and we can talk there in peace.
I'll order up three quarts of fizz, and——"

"Oh, rot your fizz!" declared Wilbur.
"If you love me, give me Christian tobacco."

As they were going out of the ballroom,
Wilbur caught sight of Josie Herrick,
and, breaking away from the others, ran
over to her.

"Oh!" she cried, breathless. "To think
and to think of your coming back after
all! No, I don't realize it—I can't. It
will take me until morning to find out
that you've really come back. I just

know now that I'm happier than I ever
was in my life before. Oh!" she cried,
"do I need to tell you how glad I am?
It's just too splendid for words. Do you
know, I was thought to be the last person
you had ever spoken to while alive, and
the reporters and all—oh, but we must
have such a talk when all are quiet again!
And our dance—we've never had our
dance. I've got your card yet. Remember the one you wrote for me at the tea—
a facsimile of it was published in all the
papers. You are going to be a hero when
you get back to San Francisco. Oh,
Ross! Ross!" she cried, the tears starting
to her eyes, "you've really come back,
and you are just as glad as I am, aren't
you—glad that you've come back—come
back to me?"

Later on, in Ridgeway's room, Wilbur
told his story again more in detail to
Ridgeway and Jerry. All but one portion of it. He could not make up his
mind to speak to them—these society

fellows, clubmen and city bred—of Moran. How he was going to order his life henceforward—his life, that he felt to be void of interest without her—he did not know. That was a question for later consideration.

"We'll give another cotillon!" exclaimed Ridgeway, "up in the city—give it for you, Ross, and you'll lead. It'll be the event of the season!"

Wilbur uttered an exclamation of contempt. "I've done with that sort of foolery," he answered.

"Nonsense; why, think, we'll have it in your honor. Every smart girl in town will come, and you'll be the lion of——"

"You don't seem to understand!" cried Wilbur impatiently. "Do you think there's any fun in that for me now? Why, man, I've fought—fought with a naked dirk, fought with a coolie who snapped at me like an ape—and you talk to me of dancing and functions and german favors! It wouldn't do some of you

17 257

people a bit of harm if you were shanghaied yourselves. That sort of life, if it don't do anything else, knocks a big bit of seriousness into you. You fellows make me sick," he went on vehemently. "As though there wasn't anything else to do but lead cotillons and get up new figures!"

"Well, what do you propose to do?" asked Nat Ridgeway. "Where are you going now—back to Magdalena Bay?"

"No."

"Where, then?"

Wilbur smote the table with his fist.

"Cuba!" he cried. "I've got a crack little schooner out in the bay here, and I've got a hundred thousand dollars' worth of loot aboard of her. I've tried beach-combing for a while, and now I'll try filibustering. It may be a crazy idea, but it's better than dancing. I'd rather lead an expedition than a german, and you can chew on that, Nathaniel Ridgeway."

Jerry looked at him as he stood there

before them in the filthy, reeking blouse
and jeans, the ragged boots, and the mane
of hair and tangled beard, and remembered
the Wilbur he used to know—the Wilbur
of the carefully creased trousers, the satin
scarfs and fancy waistcoats.

"You're a different sort than when you
went away, Ross," said Jerry.

"Right you are," answered Wilbur.

"But I will venture a prophecy," continued Jerry, looking keenly at him.
"Ross, you are a born-and-bred city man.
It's in the blood of you and the bones of
you. I'll give you three years for this
new notion of yours to wear itself out.
You think just now you're going to spend
the rest of your life as an amateur buccaneer. In three years, at the outside,
you'll be using your 'loot,' as you call it
or the interest of it, to pay your taxes
and your tailor, your pew rent and your
club dues, and you'll be what the biog-
raphers call 'a respectable member of the
community.'"

"Did you ever kill a man, Jerry?" asked Wilbur. "No? Well, you kill one some day—kill him in a fair give-and-take fight—and see how it makes you feel, and what influence it has on you, and then come back and talk to me."

It was long after midnight. Wilbur rose.

"We'll ring for a boy," said Ridgeway, "and get you a room. I can fix you out with clothes enough in the morning."

Wilbur stared in some surprise, and then said:

"Why, I've got the schooner to look after. I can't leave those coolies alone all night."

"You don't mean to say you're going on board at this time in the morning?"

"Of course!"

"Why—but—but you'll catch your death of cold."

Wilbur stared at Ridgeway, then nodded helplessly, and, scratching his head, said, half aloud:

New Conditions

"No, what's the use; I can't make 'em understand. Good-night. I'll see you in the morning."

"We'll all come out and visit you on your yacht," Ridgeway called after him; but Wilbur did not hear.

In answer to Wilbur's whistle, Jim came in with the dory and took him off to the schooner. Moran met him as he came over the side.

"I took the watch myself to-night and let the boy turn in," she said. "How is it ashore, mate?"

"We've come back to the world of little things, Moran," said Wilbur. "But we'll pull out of here in the morning and get back to the places where things are real."

"And that's a good hearing, mate."

"Let's get up here on the quarter-deck," added Wilbur. "I've something to propose to you."

Moran laid an arm across his shoulder, and the two walked aft. For half an hour Wilbur talked to her earnestly about his new idea of filibustering; and as he told her of the war he warmed to the subject, his face glowing, his eyes sparkling. Suddenly, however, he broke off.

"But no!" he exclaimed. "You don't understand, Moran. How can you—you're foreign-born. It's no affair of yours!"

"Mate! mate!" cried Moran, her hands upon his shoulders. "It's you who don't understand—don't understand me. Don't you know—can't you see? Your people are mine now. I'm happy only in your happiness. You were right—the best happiness is the happiness one shares. And your sorrows belong to me, just as I belong to you, dear. Your enemies are mine, and your quarrels are my quarrels." She drew his head quickly toward her and kissed him.

In the morning the two had made up their minds to a certain vague course of action. To get away—anywhere—was their one aim. Moran was by nature a creature unfit for civilization, and the love of adventure and the desire for action had suddenly leaped to life in Wilbur's blood and was not to be resisted.   They would get up to San Francisco, dispose of their "loot," outfit the *Bertha Millner* as a filibuster, and put to sea again.   They had discussed the advisability of rounding the Horn in so small a ship as the *Bertha Millner*, but Moran had settled that at once.

"I've got to know her pretty well," she told Wilbur.   "She's sound as a nut.   Only let's get away from this place."

But toward ten o'clock on the morning after their arrival off Coronado, and just as they were preparing to get under way, Hoang touched Wilbur's elbow.

"Seeum lil one-piece smoke-boat; him come chop-chop."

In fact, a little steam-launch was rapidly approaching the schooner.   In another instant she was alongside.   Jerry, Nat Ridgeway, Josie Herrick, and an elderly woman, whom Wilbur barely knew as Miss Herrick's married sister, were aboard.

"We've come off to see your yacht!" cried Miss Herrick to Wilbur as the launch bumped along the schooner's counter. "Can we come aboard?" She looked very pretty in her crisp pink shirt-waist, her white duck skirt, and white kid shoes, her sailor hat tilted at a barely perceptible angle. The men were in white flannels and smart yachting suits. "Can we come aboard?" she repeated.

Wilbur gasped and stared. "Good Lord!" he muttered. "Oh, come along," he added, desperately.

The party came over the side.

"Oh, my!" said Miss Herrick blankly, stopping short.

The decks, masts, and rails of the schooner were shiny with a black coating of dirt and grease; the sails were gray with grime; a strangling odor of oil and tar, of cooking and of opium, of Chinese punk and drying fish, pervaded all the

air. In the waist, Hoang and Jim, bare
to the belt, their queues looped around
their necks to be out of the way, were
stowing the dory and exchanging high-
pitched monosyllables. Miss Herrick's
sister had not come aboard. The three
visitors—Jerry, Ridgeway, and Josie—
stood nervously huddled together, their
elbows close in, as if to avoid contact
with the prevailing filth, their immaculate
white outing-clothes detaching themselves
violently against the squalor and sordid
grime of the schooner's background.

"Oh, my!" repeated Miss Herrick in
dismay, half closing her eyes. "To think
of what you must have been through! I
thought you had some kind of a yacht. I
had no idea it would be like this." And
as she spoke, Moran came suddenly upon
the group from behind the foresail, and
paused in abrupt surprise, her thumbs in
her belt.

She still wore men's clothes and was
booted to the knee. The heavy blue

woollen shirt was open at the throat, the
sleeves rolled half-way up her large white
arms. In her belt she carried her haft-
less Scandinavian dirk. She was hatless
as ever, and her heavy, fragrant cables of
rye-hued hair fell over her shoulders and
breast to far below her belt.

Miss Herrick started sharply, and
Moran turned an inquiring glance upon
Wilbur. Wilbur took his resolution in
both hands.

"Miss Herrick," he said, "this is Moran
—Moran Sternersen."

Moran took a step forward, holding out
her hand. Josie, all bewildered, put her
tight-gloved fingers into the calloused
palm, looking up nervously into Moran's
face.

"I'm sure," she said feebly, almost
breathlessly, "I — I'm sure I'm very
pleased to meet Miss Sternersen."

It was long before the picture left Wilbur's imagination. Josie Herrick, petite,
gowned in white, crisp from her maid's

grooming; and Moran, sea-rover and
daughter of an hundr. l Vikings, tower-
ing above her, booted ar l belted, gravely
clasping Josie's hand in her own huge
fist.

XIII

Moran Sternersen

SAN FRANCISCO once more! For two days the *Bertha Millner* had been beating up the coast, fighting her way against northerly winds, butting into head seas.

The warmth, the stillness, the placid, drowsing quiet of Magdalena Bay, steaming under the golden eye of a tropic heaven, the white, baked beach, the bay-heads, striated with the mirage in the morning, the coruscating sunset, the enchanted mystery of the purple night, with its sheen of stars and riding moon, were now replaced by the hale and vigorous snorting of the trades, the roll of breakers to landward, and the unremitting gallop of the unnumbered multitudes of gray-

green seas, careering silently past the
schooner, their crests occasionally hissing
into brusque eruptions of white froth, or
smiting broad on under her counter, show-
ering her decks with a spout of icy spray.
It was cold; at times thick fogs cloaked
all the world of water.   To the east, a pro-
cession of bleak hills defiled slowly southward; lighthouses were passed; streamers
of smoke on the western horizon marked
the passage of steamships; and once they
met and passed close by a huge Cape
Horner, a great deep-sea tramp, all sails
set and drawing, rolling slowly and leisurely in seas that made the schooner
dance.

At last the Farallones looked over the
ocean's edge to the north; then came the
whistling-buoy, the Seal Rocks, the
Heads, Point Reyes, the Golden Gate
flanked with the old red Presidio, Lime
Point with its watching cannon; and by
noon of a gray and boisterous day, under a
lusty wind and a slant of rain, just five

months after her departure, the *Bertha Millner* let go her anchor in San Francisco Bay some few hundred yards off the Lifeboat Station.

In this berth the schooner was still three or four miles from the city and the water-front. But Moran detested any nearer approach to civilization, and Wilbur himself was willing to avoid, at least for one day, the publicity which he believed the *Bertha's* reappearance was sure to attract. He remembered, too, that the little boat carried with her a fortune of $100,000, and decided that until it could be safely landed and stored it was not desirable that its existence should be known along "the Front."

For days, weeks even, Wilbur had looked eagerly forward to this return to his home. He had seen himself again in his former haunts, in his club, and in the houses along Pacific avenue where he was received; but no sooner had the anchor-chain ceased rattling in the *Bertha's*

hawse-pipe than a strange revulsion came
upon him.   The new man that seemed to
have so suddenly sprung to life within
him, the Wilbur who was the mate of the
Bertha Millner, the Wilbur who belonged
to Moran, believed that he could see nothing to be desired in city life.   For him was
the unsteady deck of a schooner, and the
great winds and the tremendous wheel of
the ocean's rim, and the horizon that ever
fled before his following prow; so he told
himself, so he believed.   What attractions
could the city offer him?   What amuse-
ments? what excitements?   He had been
flung off the smoothly spinning circum-
ference of well-ordered life out into the
void.

He had known romance, and the spell
of the great, simple, and primitive emo-
tions; he had sat down to eat with buc-
caneers; he had seen the fierce, quick leap
of unleashed passions, and had felt death
swoop close at his nape and pass like a
swift spurt of cold air.   City life, his old

life, had no charm for him now. Wilbur honestly believed that he was changed to his heart's core. He thought that, like Moran, he was henceforth to be a sailor of the sea, a rover, and he saw the rest of his existence passed with her, aboard their faithful little schooner. They would have the whole round world as their playground; they held the earth and the great seas in fief; there was no one to let or to hinder. They two belonged to each other. Once outside the Heads again, and they swept the land of cities and of little things behind them. and they two were left alone once more; alone in the great world of romance.

About an hour after her arrival off the station, while Hoang and the hands were furling the jib and foresail and getting the dory over the side, Moran remarked to Wilbur:

"It's good we came in when we did, mate; the glass is going down fast, and the wind's breezing up from the west;

272

we're going to have a blow; the tide will be going out in a little while, and we never could have come in against wind and tide."

"Moran," said Wilbur, "I'm going ashore—into the station here; there's a telephone line there; see the wires? I can't so much as turn my hand over before I have some shore-going clothes. What do you suppose they would do to me if I appeared on Kearney street in this outfit? I'll ring up Langley & Michaels —they are the wholesale chemists in town—and have their agent come out here and talk business to us about our ambergris. We've got to pay the men their prize - money; then as soon as we get our own money in hand we can talk about overhauling and outfitting the *Bertha*."

Moran refused to accompany him ashore and into the Lifeboat Station. Roofed houses were an object of suspicion to her. Already she had begun to be uneasy at the distant sight of the city of San Francisco, Nob, Telegraph, Russian, and Rincon hills, all swarming with buildings and grooved with streets; even the landlocked harbor fretted her. Wilbur could see she felt imprisoned, confined. When he had pointed out the Palace Hotel to her—a vast gray cube in the distance, overtopping the surrounding roofs—she had sworn under her breath.

"And people can live there, good heavens! Why not rabbit-burrows, and be done with it? Mate, how soon can we be out to sea again? I hate this place."

Wilbur found the captain of the Lifeboat Station in the act of sitting down to a dinner of boiled beef and cabbage. He was a strongly built, well-looking man, with the air more of a soldier than a sailor. He had already been studying the schooner through his front window and had recognized her, and at once asked Wilbur news of Captain Kitchell. Wilbur told him as much of his story as was

necessary, but from the captain's talk he
gathered that the news of his return had
long since been wired from Coronado, and
that it would be impossible to avoid a
nine-days' notoriety. The captain of the
station (his name was Hodgson) made
Wilbur royally welcome, insisted upon
his dining with him, and himself called
up Langley & Michaels as soon as the
meal was over.

It was he who offered the only plausi-
ble solution of the mystery of the lifting
and shaking of the schooner and the
wrecking of the junk. Though Wilbur
was not satisfied with Hodgson's explanation, it was the only one he ever
heard.

When he had spoken of the matter,
Hodgson had nodded his head. "Sulphur-
bottoms," he said.

"Sulphur-bottoms?"

"Yes; they're a kind of right whale;
they get barnacles and a kind of marine
lice on their backs, and come up and

scratch themselves against a ship's keel
just like a hog under a fence."

When Wilbur's business was done, and
he was making ready to return to the
schooner, Hodgson remarked suddenly:
"Hear you've got a strapping fine girl
aboard with you. Where did you fall in
with her?" and he winked and grinned.

Wilbur started as though struck, and
took himself hurriedly away; but the
man's words had touched off in his brain
a veritable mine of conjecture. Moran
in Magdalena Bay was consistent, congruous, and fitted into her environment.
But how—how was Wilbur to explain her
to San Francisco, and how could his be-
havior seem else than ridiculous to the
men of his club and to the women whose
dinner invitations he was wont to receive?
They could not understand the change
that had been wrought in him; they did
not know Moran, the savage, half-tamed
Valkyrie so suddenly become a woman.
Hurry as he would, the schooner could

not be put to sea again within a fortnight.
Even though he elected to live aboard in
the mean while, the very business of her
preparation would call him to the city
again and again. Moran could not be
kept a secret. As it was, all the world
knew of her by now. On the other hand,
he could easily understand her position;
to her it seemed simplicity itself that they
two who loved each other should sail away
and pass their lives together upon the sea,
as she and her father had done before.

Like most men, Wilbur had to walk
when he was thinking hard. He sent the
dory back to the schooner with word to
Moran that he would take a walk around
the beach and return in an hour or two.
He set off along the shore in the direction of Fort Mason, the old red-brick fort
at the entrance to the Golden Gate. At
this point in the Presidio Government
reservation the land is solitary. Wilbur
followed the line of the beach to the old
fort; and there on the very threshold of

the Western world, at the very outpost of civilization, sat down in the lee of the crumbling fortification, and scene by scene reviewed the extraordinary events of the past six months.

In front of him ran the narrow channel of the Golden Gate; to his right was the bay and the city; at his left, the open Pacific.

He saw himself the day of his advent aboard the *Bertha* in his top hat and frock coat; saw himself later "braking down" at the windlass, the *Petrel* within hailing distance.

Then the pictures began to thicken fast: the derelict bark, *Lady Letty*, rolling to her scuppers, abandoned and lonely; the "boy" in the wheel-box; Kitchell wrenching open the desk in the captain's stateroom; Captain Sternersen buried at sea, his false teeth upside down; the black fury of the squall, and Moran at the wheel; Moran lying at full length on the deck, getting the altitude of a star; Magdalena

Bay; the shark-fishing; the mysterious
lifting and shuddering of the schooner;
the beachcombers' junk, with its staring
red eyes; Hoang, naked to the waist,
gleaming with sweat and whale-oil; the
ambergris; the race to beach the sinking
schooner; the never-to-be-forgotten night
when he and Moran had camped together
on the beach; Hoang taken prisoner, and
the hideous filing of his teeth; the beachcombers, silent and watchful behind their
sand breastworks; the Chinaman he had
killed twitching and hiccoughing at his
feet; Moran turned Bersark, bursting
down upon him through a haze of smoke;
Charlie dying in the hammock aboard the
schooner, ordering his funeral with its
"four-piecee horse"; Coronado; the in-
congruous scene in the ballroom; and, last
of all, Josie Herrick in white duck and
kid shoes, giving her hand to Moran in
her boots and belt, hatless as ever, her
sleeves rolled up to above the elbows, her
white, strong arm extended, her ruddy

face, and pale, milk-blue eyes gravely observant, her heavy braids, yellow as ripen-
ing rye, hanging over shoulder and breast.

A sudden explosion of cold wind, striking down blanket-wise and bewildering
from out the west, made Wilbur look up
quickly. The gray sky seemed scudding
along close overhead. The bay, the narrow channel of the Golden Gate, the outside ocean, were all whitening with crests
of waves. At his feet the huge green
ground-swells thundered to the attack of
the fort's granite foundations. Through
the Gate, the bay seemed rushing out
to the Pacific. A bewildered gull shot
by, tacking and slanting against the gusts
that would drive it out to sea. Evidently
the storm was not far off. Wilbur rose to
his feet, and saw the *Bertha Millner*, close
in, unbridled and free as a runaway horse,
headed directly for the open sea, and rushing on with all the impetus of wind and
tide!

XIV

The Ocean Is Calling for You

A LITTLE while after Wilbur had set off from the station, while Moran was making the last entries in the log-book, seated at the table in the cabin, Jim appeared at the door.

"Well," she said, looking up.

"China boy him want go asho' plenty big, seeum flen up Chinatown in um city."

"Shore leave, is it?" said Moran. "You deserted once before without even saying good-by; and my hand in the fire, you'll come back this time dotty with opium. Get away with you. We'll have men aboard here in a few days."

"Can go?" inquired Jim suavely.

"I said so. Report our arrival to your Six Companies."

Hoang rowed Jim and the coolies ashore, and then returned to the schooner with the dory and streamed her astern. As he passed the cabin door on his way forward, Moran hailed him.

"I thought you went ashore?" she cried.

"Heap flaid," he answered. "Him other boy go up Chinatown; him tell Sam Yup; I tink Sam Yup alla same killee me. I no leaveum ship two, thlee day; bimeby I go Olegon. I stay topside ship. You wantum cook, I cook plenty fine; standum watch for you."

Indeed, ever since leaving Coronado the ex-beachcomber had made himself very useful about the schooner; had been, in fact, obsequiousness itself, and seemed to be particularly desirous of gaining the good-will of the *Bertha's* officers. He understood pigeon English better than Jim, and spoke it even better than Charlie had done. He acted the part of interpre-

ter between Wilbur and the hands; even
turned to in the galley upon occasion; and
of his own accord offered to give the vessel a coat of paint above the water-line.
Moran turned back to her log, and Hoang
went forward. Standing on the forward
deck, he looked after the *Bertha's* coolies
until they disappeared behind a row of
pine-trees on the Presidio Reservation,
going cityward. Wilbur was nowhere in
sight. For a long time Hoang studied the
Lifeboat Station narrowly, while he made
a great show of coiling a length of rope.
The station was just out of hailing distance. Nobody seemed stirring. The
whole shore and back land thereabouts
was deserted; the edge of the city was
four miles distant. Hoang returned to
the forecastle-hatch and went below,
groping under his bunk in his ditty-box.

"Well, what is it?" exclaimed Moran a
moment later, as the beachcomber entered
the cabin and shut the door behind him.

Hoang did not answer; but she did not

need to repeat the question. In an instant Moran knew very well what he had come for.

"God!" she exclaimed under her breath, springing to her feet. "Why didn't we think of this!"

Hoang slipped his knife from the sleeve of his blouse. For an instant the old imperiousness, the old savage pride and anger, leaped again in Moran's breast— then died away forever. She was no longer the same Moran of that first fight on board the schooner, when the beachcombers had plundered her of her "loot." Only a few weeks ago, and she would have fought with Hoang without hesitation and without mercy; would have wrenched a leg from the table and brained him where he stood. But she had learned since to know what it meant to be dependent; to rely for protection upon some one who was stronger than she; to know her weakness; to know that she was at last a woman, and to be proud of it.

The Ocean Is Calling for You

She did not fight; she had no thought of fighting. Instinctively she cried aloud, "Mate—mate! Oh, mate, where are you? Help me!" and Hoang's knife nailed the words within her throat.

The "loot" was in a brass-bound chest under one of the cabin's bunks, stowed in two gunny-bags. Hoang drew them out, knotted the two together, and, slinging them over his shoulder, regained the deck.

He looked carefully at the angry sky and swelling seas, noting the direction of the wind and set of the tide; then went forward and cast the anchor-chains from the windlass in such a manner that the schooner must inevitably wrench free with the first heavy strain. The dory was still tugging at the line astern. Hoang dropped the sacks in the boat, swung himself over the side, and rowed calmly toward the station's wharf. If any notion of putting to sea with the schooner had entered the obscure, perverted cunning of his mind, he had almost instantly rejected it.

Chinatown was his aim; once there and under the protection of his tong, Hoang knew that he was safe. He knew the hiding-places that the See Yup Association provided for its members—hiding-places whose very existence was unknown to the police of the White Devil.

No one interrupted—no one even noticed—his passage to the station. At best, it was nothing more than a coolie carrying a couple of gunny-sacks across his shoulder. Two hours later, Hoang was lost in San Francisco's Chinatown.

. . . . . .

At the sight of the schooner sweeping out to sea, Wilbur was for an instant smitten rigid. What had happened? Where was Moran? Why was there nobody on board? A swift, sharp sense of some unnamed calamity leaped suddenly at his throat. Then he was aware of a clattering of hoofs along the road that led to the fort. Hodgson threw himself from one of the horses that were used in handling the surf-boat, and ran to him hatless and panting.

"My God!" he shouted. "Look, your schooner, do you see her? She broke away after I'd started to tell you—to tell you—to tell you—your girl there on board—— It was horrible!"

"Is she all right?" cried Wilbur, at top voice, for the clamor of the gale was increasing every second.

"All right! No; they've killed her—somebody—the coolies, I think—knifed her! I went out to ask you people to come into the station to have supper with me——"

"Killed her—killed her! Who? I don't believe you——"

"Wait—to have supper with me, and I found her there on the cabin floor. She was still breathing. I carried her up on deck—there was nobody else aboard. I

carried her up and laid her on the deck—
and she died there. Just now I came
after you to tell you, and——"

"Good God Almighty, man! who killed
her? Where is she? Oh—but of course
it isn't true! How did you know? Moran killed! Moran killed!"

"And the schooner broke away after I
started!"

"Moran killed! But—but—she's not
dead yet; we'll have to see——"

"She died on the deck; I brought her
up and laid her on——"

"How do you know she's dead? Where
is she? Come on, we'll go right back to
her—to the station!"

"She's on board—out there!"

"Where — where is she? My God,
man, tell me where she is!"

"Out there aboard the schooner. I
brought her up on deck—I left her on
the schooner—on the deck—she was
stabbed in the throat—and then came
after you to tell you. Then the schooner

288

broke away while I was coming; she's drifting out to sea now!"

"Where is she? Where is she?"

"Who—the girl—the schooner—which one? The girl is on the schooner—and the schooner—that's her, right there—she's drifting out to sea!"

Wilbur put both hands to his temples, closing his eyes.

"I'll go back!" exclaimed Hodgson. "We'll have the surf-boat out and get after her; we'll bring the body back!"

"No, no!" cried Wilbur, "it's better—this way. Leave her, let her go—she's going out to sea—out to sea again!"

"But the schooner won't live two hours outside in this weather; she'll go down!"

"It's better—that way—let her go. I want it so!"

"I can't stay! I can't stay here!" said the other. "There's a storm coming up, and I've got to be at my station."

Wilbur did not answer; he was watching the schooner.

"I can't stay!" cried the other again.
"If the patrol should signal—I can't stop
here, I must be on duty. Come back,
you can't do anything!"

"No!"

"I have got to go!" Hodgson ran back,
swung himself on the horse, and rode away
at a furious gallop, inclining his head
against the gusts.

And the schooner in a world of flying
spray, white scud, and driving spoondrift,
her cordage humming, her forefoot churning, the flag at her peak straining stiff in
the gale, came up into the narrow passage
of the Golden Gate, riding high upon the
outgoing tide. On she came, swinging
from crest to crest of the waves that
kept her company, and that ran to meet
the ocean, shouting and calling out
beyond there under the low, scudding
clouds.

Wilbur had climbed to the top of the
old fort. Erect upon its granite ledge he
stood, and watched and waited.

The Ocean Is Calling for You

Not once did the *Bertha Millner* falter in her race. Like an unbitted horse, all restraint shaken off, she ran free toward the ocean as to her pasture-land. She came nearer, nearer, rising and rolling with the seas, her bowsprit held due west, pointing like a finger out to sea, to the west—out to the world of romance. And then at last, as the little vessel drew opposite the old fort and passed not one hundred yards away, Wilbur, watching from the rampart, saw Moran lying upon the deck with outstretched arms and calm, upturned face; lying upon the deck of that lonely fleeing schooner as upon a bed of honor, still and calm, her great braids smooth upon her breast, her arms wide; alone with the sea: alone in death as she had been in life. She passed out of his life as she had come into it—alone, upon a derelict ship, abandoned to the sea. She went out with the tide, out with the storm; out, out, out to the great gray Pacific that knew her and loved her, and that shouted and called for her, and thundered in the joy of her as she came to meet him like a bride to meet a bridegroom.

"Good-by, Moran!" shouted Wilbur as she passed. "Good-by, good-by, Moran! You were not for me—not for me! The ocean is calling for you, dear; don't you hear him? Don't you hear him? Good-by, good-by, good-by!"

The schooner swept by, shot like an arrow through the swirling currents of the Golden Gate, and dipped and bowed and courtesied to the Pacific that reached toward her his myriad curling fingers. They enfolded her, held her close, and drew her swiftly, swiftly out to the great heaving bosom, tumultuous and beating in its mighty joy, its savage exultation of possession.

Wilbur stood watching. The little schooner lessened in the distance—became a shadow in mist and flying spray— a shadow moving upon the face of the great waste of water. Fainter and fainter she grew, vanished, reappeared, was heaved up again—a mere speck upon the western sky—a speck that dwindled and dwindled, then slowly melted away into the gray of the horizon.

THE END